Solstice Publishing Presents

Summer Thrills
Summer Chills

Cover Art:
Michelle Crocker

http://mlcdesigns4you.weebly.com/

Publisher's Note:

This is a work of fiction. All names, characters, places, and events are the work of the author's imagination.

Any resemblance to real persons, places, or events is coincidental.

Solstice Publishing - www.solsticepublishing.com

Table of Contents:

The Ghost of Camp Linnenmyer
S Cu'Anam

I dedicate this story to the Campers of Camp
Lindenmere 1994-1998.
To Catherine Shegda Wolfe, who always helped me
along on whatever adventure my brain created.
To Dana Caruso, who once said, "It's not going to
explode" as she held a lighter to a can of spray paint behind
Stone Lodge.
And to Mike Scharff, the man who first asked me
the question "Who is John Galt?" R.I.P. Old man
***

I was thirteen the year my grandparents decided to
send me to Camp Linnenmyer. It was a sleep away camp in
the Pocono Mountains, far from any sign of civilization. I
did not want to go. I had never been off my block, let alone
out of my state before.

"It'll do you good to get out of New York for a few
weeks, Shanala," my grandmother stated. I cringed
inwardly as she called me by my Hebrew name. She only
called me Shanala when she was buttering me up.

"But Gram, I won't know anyone there. And I'll
get made fun of because I'm not rich like the other kids," I
complained.

That part was at least true. I was far from rich. My
grandparents were, but my mother was the black sheep of
the family. I guess that made me the black lamb? Who
knows. I just knew there would be issues if anyone at this
place figured out I lived in the ghetto.

I chanced a glance outside to the snow-covered
concrete and tar, the mid-January air hitting me like a
whipe from the crack in the window. My vision was marred
by the black iron bars that were laid like a fence over every
window in my second floor apartment. They said it was to
protect us from falling out, but to me they looked like the
bars on prison cells. Hardly anyone who was born here ever
got out. The whole neighborhood was like one massive

prison, built to hold us sorry saps within its walls. That's how I felt about it anyway. Then again I was thirteen. And a half. What did I know about anything?

My mother—she was oblivious to everything. All she did was sit and stare between us with this blank expression as if she had no idea what was going on. The vacant look mingled with her not telling them to let me stay home almost made me want to slap the life back into her. I knew the consequences of that though. I had enough bruises in places no one could see without really looking as a testimony to that.

I was resigned to my fate. I gave a heavy sigh and hung my head. "Fine. I'll go."

My grandmother gave a brilliant smile. She could sell ice to Eskimos with her smile. "You'll see Shanala, this summer will be the best of your life."

The months passed in the same blur as they always did. When you live where I did, color was almost a mystery, everything seemed to be in the dullest shades of grey. They had done the gentrification thing, fencing off the small patches that grass and planting more trees. To me, it only served to make our "projects" look more like the prison it was meant to be.

I would be leaving at the end of June, the day after school let out for the summer. I had survived my first year of high school with a B average. At least I could be proud of that. Not many where I was from even graduated, let alone did well.

The day before I was to leave, I saw my grandparents' beige Impala pull up. My grandfather, who had disowned my mother. As always, he refused to get out of the car, so my grandmother called up to me from outside. I flew out of the house, the blue painted metal door that marked the entrance to my apartment slamming shut behind me. I raced down the mocha-painted steps sounding like a herd of elephants; at least that was my mother's

6

favorite phrase to use. After fighting the magnetic lock on the apartment building door, I flung it open and hugged my grandmother.

"I don't leave until tomorrow, Gram. You're a day early," I giggled as I released my hold on her frail form.

"We're taking you shopping to get you ready for tomorrow, Shanala," my grandmother replied with a smile.

I guess my face must have lit up since hers got even brighter. Our moment was short lived though as my grandfather in his impatience, and hatred of where my mother chose to live, honked the horn and called. "Let's go Beatrice, we haven't got all day!"

My grandmother ruffled my shoulder length auburn hair. As we walked to the car I whispered. "What did she do to piss him off this time?" My grandmother never answered.

Three hours and eight hundred dollars later, my brand new trunk was all packed and ready to go.

I spent the rest of the afternoon sitting outside my building talking to my friend Babs. We were best friends until that summer. I did the whole girly crying thing, and swore to write to each other every day for the entire eight weeks I would be gone.

Babs looked at me seriously. "Promise you'll tell me about all the cute guys there!"

I nodded. "Okay, but you have to keep me up to date about here. I won't be able to read the Police Blotter to see who got caught or shot so I'll be clueless."

As if on cue, a blue and white patrol car raced passed us with its sirens blaring, loudly. Babs covered her ears like she always did and gave an exasperated "Ugh!" when it had passed.

I arched a brow at my own realization. "I have no idea how I'll sleep out there without all the noise of the city!" This made Babs laugh.

As the street lights began to come on one at a time,

we hugged and cried again and said goodbye. Then I headed upstairs.

Dinner was uneventful. It always was. I glanced at the macaroni and cheese my fork was stabbing to death and prayed silently that there would be more variety and better food at the camp. Despite my apprehension about going to Camp Linnenmyer, I found that sleep eluded me at every turn. As a last ditch effort, I pulled my softball jersey to me to try to get some form of comfort, my trusty teddy bear lay beside me.

At the normal time that the strange and unusual happened, I heard the right closet door pop as it unstuck from the frame, then creak open slowly. It's happened every night for as long as I could remember, yet it always made the hairs on my arm stand on end. The closet door opened six inches and stopped, just like it always did. I don't know why, but I cast a glance to the hand threaded jack in the box picture that hung on my wall. It was in cahoots with the closet. I swear it to this day, twenty years later. I drew my blanket tighter to me as I watched the jack start to sway in his box. "At least I'll be rid of whatever you are for eight weeks," was my last coherent thought.

My grandparents arrived to collect me and my trunk at exactly six in the morning. I half-pulled, half-dragged the heavy trunk down the stairs.

"Shanala, it would be easier if you took the elevator," my grandmother pointed out, to which I glared at the evil moving box. I had gotten stuck in that thing twice and they had had to pry the doors open with the Jaws of Life the second time. Fat chance of me of ever getting in there again.

"I'm fine Gram," I grunted, stubborn as ever.

The car ride to Carnarsie was uneventful. My grandfather had classical music droning out of the Impala's speakers. I stared out the window watching the world flash by, trying not to get car sick. With all the stuff we had gotten at the store yesterday, none of us had thought to pick up a bottle of Dramamine for my nasty habit of getting motion sickness.

There were so many cars parked at the drop off spot, that we had to park six blocks away in what I dubbed "No Man's Land." My grandparents were spry, considering, but my new teen standards they were positively ancient and had roamed with the dinosaurs. The fact that I was the only kid I knew whose grandparents were as old as everyone's great grandparents did little to change my opinion on this topic. The Coach bus stop was swarming with kids from the wealthier parts of New York. Of course there was not a single face there that I knew. I turned to ask my grandparents if they would stay until the bus came, but they were already on half a block away. I sighed, more than a little depressed as I looked around at all the parents hugging and talking with their kids. I planted myself on my trunk and felt like an absolute freak since I was there all by myself.

My hazel eyes lit up as the bus that would shuttle us to the Camp pulled into its bay. It was magnificent really. It had to be bigger than any bus I had ever seen, which was not saying much since the only buses I ever saw were the city transit buses. I was awed as I climbed onto the bus. My jaw hit the thin carpet on the walkway as my eyes roamed over the thick cushioned seats and the windows with curtains! I took a seat toward the front of the bus, since everyone else seemed to like to sit like a can of sardines in the back. I looked out the window and watched a man, I assumed a counselor, place my trunk under the bus. As the bus pulled out of its docking bay, I felt a small twinge of sorrow fill me, but I quickly swallowed it, wondering why I was so upset when no one cared if I was leaving. The thought only made me more upset and I hummed in frustration as I felt the first tear hit my CD player.

The drive was boring. It took us hours to get there. Civilization was long gone and the road—yes, road, I'm not even sure there was asphalt on it—was surrounded by trees on both sides. I quickly noted the lack of street lights which would make this place pitch black when the sun set.

We were told we were about five minutes from Camp Linnenmyre when the bus hit something large and hard and I whacked my head on the seat in front of me. We all began to regain our bearings, sitting up and picking stuff off the floor. I rubbed the massive welt forming on my forehead as I tried to peak out the window to see what we could have hit. A massive felled tree barred our way from going any further. Movement from the corner of my eye had me turn my head. I caught a glimpse of man-sized white fur disappear into the trees. I rubbed my eyes, thinking I had imagined it when a girl sitting behind me spoke.

"Hey! Did you see that?" she asked, sounding shocked.

I turned in my seat to look at her. She was taller than I was, her glasses making her look older than me. "See what?" I asked, feigning ignorance.

"That flash of fur. I know you saw it—your eyes almost popped out of your head."

I nodded slowly. "Does stuff like that happen a lot here?"

"Nah. Not usually. At least not while I've been here. We could ask my mom though. She's the camp nurse. She knows all kinds of things about this place. By the way, my name's Cat." She stuck a hand out in my direction.

"Shirley," I replied, accepting the proffered hand and giving it a shake before continuing. "How long have you been coming here?"

Cat thought a minute before replying. "Since I was five, so seven years now. Almost eight. My birthday's in July."

Just then the bus lurched forward. As we drove past, I saw the moss covered tree laying idly on the side of the road.

Five minutes later, and half an hour late, our bus joined five others on a large soccer field. At the field's side line was a basketball court, and about twenty feet from there, a wooden house.

Cat and I waited for everyone else to get off the bus before we did. As we stepped onto the damp grass, Cat must have noticed my staring at the wooden structure. "That's BB3," she stated.

"BB3?" I asked, arching a brow.

Cat nodded. "Mhm, Boys Bunk 3."

"Lame. Are the girls' bunks named like that too?" I asked.

Cat shook her head. "No. All of our bunks except three are named for people in the book *Atlas Shrugged* by Ayn Rand. Half of the boys' bunks are named for places in the book."

I gave her a blank expression, one I'm sure would have reminded anyone who knew me of my mother.

"You'll figure it out sooner or later. Come on, I'll show you around." Cat said, taking me by my upper arm and pulling me away from the bus.

"Um..Shouldn't we go where everyone else is?" I asked pointing behind us. Everyone was taking seats on the basketball court we'd passed.

"They won't miss us. They probably won't even notice we're gone," Cat assured me as we came to stop at what looked to me like a furniture graveyard. There were broken chairs, beds, and all kinds of other things piled up in a vacant space of yellow grass between BB3 and the adjacent forest.

I looked around, confused. "Why are we here?"

"Shhh. Be quiet and you'll find out," Cat said in a hushed voice.

Against my better judgement, I stood there. The mountain air pushed passed us in a light breeze. I could not hear or see or even feel whatever it was Cat wanted from me. In fact, she was starting to make me uncomfortable.

I was just about to tell this strange kid that I was going to go and join the others when the hairs on my arm stood on end. A strange sense of foreboding overtook me. I had no idea why, but as soon as that I had felt whatever it was, I was scared out of my mind. I cast my gaze frantically around the woods but there was nothing there. My heart was thudding in my chest, and my breaths were hurried. I still had no idea why I was so afraid.

A twig snapped somewhere in the woods, causing me to gasp and jump about a foot in the air. Then I saw him. A man, his skin the color of fine tanned leather. His hair was ebony and almost to his waist. He was dressed head to toe in cured white wolf fur, the hollowed out head of a white wolf a helmet on his head. He never spoke a word, but his gaze pierced through to my soul. Even as we stood watching him, he faded away until he was gone.

"What was that?!" I nearly screamed at Cat. I was ready to bolt back onto the bus and demand that the driver take me home. I could deal with gangs and drug dealers. I knew those things. Ghosts were a whole other ballgame.

Cat laughed. Outright laughed at me! I felt my face grow red, whether from embarrassment or anger I do not know. Perhaps it was just a mix of both. "Relax. My mom can tell you about him. She knows everything about the tribes out here."

We walked back the way we had come. The buses were gone. So was everyone else. Cat had been right, no one had noticed we were not there. As we neared the actual entrance to the camp, I noted my trunk sitting on the porch of a two story bunkhouse with stone steps.

"Oh! Looks like we'll be bunking together! Welcome to High View." Cat smiled as we turned up a wide, steep hilled, gravel road.

"High View?" I huffed. I already knew this road would be my death. "Why is it called High View?"

Cat shrugged. "Cause it's high up, I guess. It used to have another name, but it got renamed after the CiTs lived there for a summer." She must have seen my look when she said CiT because she answered before I could even ask. "CiT—Counselor in Training. Basically kids four years older than us that think they can do whatever they want since they'll be counselors next year."

"Oh." Somehow I knew this was not going to sit well with me.

We finally crested the mountain of the gravel road and Cat pointed to a trail off to the right. It was almost hidden with overgrowth.

"That's where the CiTs stay now.. Stone Lodge. We aren't supposed to go in there though. They'd kill us 'cause you know they think we're little kids. But Stone Lodge is the coolest bunk in the whole camp. It was cool before Linnenmyer was a camp at all actually." Cat explained.

I looked confused, my gaze transferring between the hidden trail and Cat. "Before it was a camp?"

Cat nodded. "This place used to be a ski lodge like fifty years ago. Until Mike bought it and turned it into a camp. Stone Lodge, High View, and the Main House are the only buildings here from back then. All the others were built when they turned it into a camp."

After what felt like hours of walking, and Cat rambling about the camp's history, we came upon a long building with a ramp on either side of the double doors.

"What's this place?" I asked as we started up the ramp to the left.

Cat smiled. "Mess Hall. It's dinner time."

Dinner consisted of the worst pizza I had ever tasted. It was Elio's pizza and everyone knows not even people where I lived would eat it. For as bad as the pizza was,-whoever cooked it that night had given me new reason to wish for my mother's soupy macaroni and cheese. The cheese was practically glued to the underside of the slice under it. Yes, yes, they had piled the square slices up like brownies. And the pizza itself tasted like its cardboard box. Well, the cardboard box probably tasted better honestly.

After I reminded myself that if I did not eat, I would starve to death, I wolfed down two slices of the rubbery cardboard, then followed Cat back toward our side of the camp. We passed a huge blue and white painted rock and Cat stopped briefly to pat it.

Seeing my questioning look she explained. "Linnenmyre Rock. It's been here in this spot as long as anyone can remember." I gave a nod as we continued on.

We passed High View and continued on angling toward the Infirmary. We circled the building to the back and Cat pushed the door open. "Hi Mom! I brought a friend!" Cat called out as she ushered me into the room. That's all it was really, a room with a dresser and a bed, but it was decorated in dream catchers, mandalas, and all kinds of other Native décor. I could not help myself as I looked over everything in awe, before my eyes fell a woman who without a doubt was Cat's mother, but was native herself somewhere in her line.

"Hi." I said shyly as I found myself unable to look this woman in the face.

"Mom, this is Shirley, Shirley, this is my mom Pauline. She can answer your questions, I'm sure of it," Cat said enthusiastically.

I groaned inwardly. I had no intention of talking to this woman, who I did not know, about the strange things that seem to find me no matter where I am.

"Cat, are you sure she wanted to talk to me?" Pauline asked, almost reprimanding her daughter.

"It's okay, really. I saw an Indi—I mean a Native

in the woods. Twice today. The second time he vanished into thin air." I stammered nervously.

Pauline shifted from her seat on her bed. "Do you things like that a lot, Shirley?"

I debated a few seconds on whether or not to tell the truth concerning this, then sighed. "Not that one. But others. A lot."

Pauline nodded. Her brow furrowed in thought as I watched. "Do you ever see any animals? Not ones you can reach out and touch, but ones you see in peripheral?"

I did not hesitate this time as I answered. "Wolves. Three of them. One massive and red, one small and black, one small and grey."

Pauline's next question had me thinking I should probably be admitted to the nearest mental ward. "Have they told you their names yet?"

I shifted uncomfortably. "Red, Tam Tur, and Laurel."

Then Pauline did something no one else had ever done. She did not humor me, or mock me. She pointed by my feet. "Laurel." Then she pointed by Cat. "Tam." And finally she pointed to the closed door. "Red is outside guarding."

I blinked and looked into Pauline's eyes finally. "You can see them!" It was a statement, not a question. I had no doubt Cat's mother saw all three wolves since she pointed to each one and said their names.

Her nod confirmed it. "There are few left in the world that haven't closed their minds off to the other planes of existence. You, Shirley, are one of them. It's getting late, you girls should head back to your bunk. Heed this warning Shirley, out here where the Shawnee rest, be careful. Brave Wolf won't be able to drive the evil off all the time. He can't be everywhere at once."

I felt a shiver race down my spine despite the heat and nodded my head as I followed Cat out.

Lights out was not for another hour. I was sitting on my bed which I had just finished making with my new sheets. My bed was in the far back corner of the bunk. Cat's was next to mine. I flopped onto the bed and looked up to the raftered roof. And spied a small ball of brown fur that looked wedged in the corner. I grabbed my flashlight and stood on my bed and cast the beam on the darkened corner. The brown ball moved a bit, little leathery wings unfurled before curling back against the ball. "A bat!" I almost squealed in excitement. This had to be the smallest bat I had ever heard of; well, then again, for all I knew it was the size of all bats. I had never seen a bat before now.

Just then, Sumi, our councilor, walked by and hissed. "Hey kid! Stop standing your bed!" I had learned her name—was it really so hard for her to learn mine? I was about to ask but when I turned to face her, her eyes flashed blood red. I gasped and slid into a sitting position on my bed.

When Sumi was gone, Cat looked at me and asked quietly, "Are you okay? You look a bit pale. Maybe a little green around the gills."

I looked to Cat. I had felt my body temperature plummet when I had looked at Sumi, so I figured she was right in how pale I was. "Her eyes were red!" I said in a hissed whisper. I would have pretty much given anything for whatever was in my closet that made the jack in the box picture move at that point. I was done with the camp experience.

Cat's gaze hardened. I know she believed me simply because we had both seen Brave Wolf, and there was no way I could even contemplate a lie like that and pull it off. "We can't tell my mom. She'd throw a fit and leave. We'll deal with this on our own. I'll have a plan worked out in the morning."

I discovered morning for us was about ninety minutes before the sun rose. Half frozen, and still groggy, I dragged my feet toward the Mess Hall.

"You've got the zombie shuffle down flawlessly, Shirl." Cat joked.

I looked up to her through bloodshot eyes and muttered something that even to my ears sounded zombie-like. Ugh! I had not even been here a full day yet!

I moved my frosted flakes around in the little plastic self-serve bowl without having taken a single bite. My gaze was locked expectantly on Cat, who instead of telling me this brilliant plan of hers was munching on her second self-serve bowl of Cheerios.

"Well?!" I finally asked, getting aggravated with her deliberate delay in saying anything.

Cat shook her head and swallowed the last spoonful of Cheerios. "Not here. Too many ears. We'll talk when we go to the lake for Nature."

We left the Mess Hall with everyone else. While all the other girls in our bunk chittered and giggled and cast sidelong glances at the boys in our age group, Cat and myself trudged on in silence. We reached High View and climbed the stairs to the second floor where our bunks were. We both stopped dead in our tracks. Scrawled across the wall in dripping red were the words "Leave Now."

I held a hand to my nose as the stench in the room finally invaded my senses. "Oh my God! What *is* that?!"

Cat, pinching her nostrils together with her left hand, walked up to the writing and looked at it. As if it were an afterthought she asked. "Did you see that shy girl Melissa at breakfast?"

I blinked and shook my head. "Nu-uh. Sumi wasn't there either."

Cat nodded and headed back down the stairs. I started to follow, but something made me look back. I felt my heart twist and my breakfast, what little I had picked at, tried to make a reappearance. A small brown furred ball lay motionless on my pillow. "I'm sorry Batty," I whispered so softly I barely the words as I choked back a sob and ran down the stairs.

We went to the Main House and told Mike what we had discovered. He scratched his balding head. He had to be at least as old as my grandparents.

After a few minutes, he nodded. "You girls head on down to the lake for your class. We'll have everything cleaned up when you get back."

Just before the door closed behind us we heard Mike say into his phone, "It's happened again."

We crossed the road leaving the camp for the woods and the wide trail that would take us to the lake. I started down the trail which was wide enough for a tank to roll down, until Cat touched my shoulder and stopped me.

"Come this way. It's quieter and we'll be able to talk," Cat said as she headed down a narrow path almost totally hidden by poison ivy.

"Cat. We'll get rashes." I was as I followed her.

"I'm immune. Poison ivy isn't really poison. It's just an allergy. You have to be allergic to it to get a rash." Cat explained.

I nodded and followed, praying with each step that the silver bottomed leaves were not something I was allergic to. We were halfway down the path when I heard a gentle rumbling sound. Loose dirt and small pebbles began to bounce around and tremble. I knew it was not an earthquake, we were on the wrong side of the country for those. Then I saw the cause of the ruckus. A herd of deer. One buck and four does bounding through the woods like something was chasing them. The buck stopped and looked at us for a moment and then leapt. The does followed and as soon as all five had left the ground, they vanished into thin air. A lone wolf howled mournfully after the specters. A shudder escaped me as we continued on our way. Neither of us spoke about the ghost herd, though from the look on Cat's face, this was something that did not occur every day.

The trail opened out to the other side of a large lake. This was possibly the largest man-made lake I would ever see, complete with its own step stone waterfall. It did not take us long to figure out we were not alone. Sitting at the edge of the lake holding a reed with fishing line tied to it was a girl. She would be considered overweight by most but I thought she looked fine the way she was. I recognized her as one of the girls who shared the second floor of High View with us.

"Dana," Cat mumbled.

"Cat," Dana replied.

You could slice the tension in the air with a knife it was that thick. I shifted my weight from foot to foot, beginning to feel uncomfortable.

"You must be the new kid. The other girls keep asking each other how you're here. They said you don't smell rich," Dana said with a shrug.

I felt my hands ball into fists and did not even try to brush the strands of hair that had fallen in my eyes away.

"Don't worry about Blair and them. They're snobs anyway. I don't care if you're rich or live in a box," Dana said with a chuckle. This did not ease my mood nor my mind.

Cat grew impatient. "Why are you down here, Dana?"

"I wanted to go to Turtle Island, but Liam won't let us use the paddle boats or the canoes. He's over there droning on about fireflies." Dana answered with a roll of her deep brown eyes.

Turtle Island was a shallow end of the lake opposite from where were stood. None of the boats could get fully across that side of the lake and you'd have to walk in the lake on that side. Mind you, this is not ideal in a lake full of leeches or snap turtles. But the snap turtles were what gave that side of the lake its name. There were tons of them over there.

"What are you two doing here? And why did you take that trail? You know if you get caught you'll get in trouble," Dana questioned.

Cat rolled her eyes. "Look I'm only going to tell you this because my mom likes you and you aren't *that* bad. Something's going on around here."

Dana arched her brow. "You aren't going to start with that whole 'there's ghosts in the camp' crap again, are you?"

"It's true!" I said before my brain registered that my mouth had moved without its permission.

Dana looked at Cat incredulously. "You got to her already? She's only been here for like a day!"

"Cat didn't get to anything. I saw it before I met Cat on the bus. I saw Brave Wolf twice, and ghost deer, and someone killed Batty!" Clearly the stress of the last twenty- four hours had finally caught up to me. I heard my voice crack before I felt the tears trickle down my cheeks.

Dana looked to Cat and mouthed "Who's Batty?"

I'd seen it and replied, "He was the bat that slept in the rafters above my bed. I saw him dead on my pillow after we saw the words in blood on the wall between mine and Cat's beds."

Dana blinked.

"When we told Mike, he muttered into his phone that it was happening again," Cat added.

Dana thought a minute. You could almost see the light bulb turn on above her head. "I think he's referring to the incident that forced the lodge to close. You know he got

I slipped out of my sneakers and busied myself with stepping on the waterfall steps as the two talked. I was paying enough attention to ask, "What happened that the lodge closed?"

It was Cat who answered. "A girl drowned in Stone Lodge."

That stopped me in my tracks. "How did someone

drown in a ski lodge?" I asked, confused.

"Her name was Heather Mason. She and her fiancé Anthony had decided to get married at the lodge since they had first met here. They say she was in the basement of Stone Lodge, trying on her wedding gown, but never showed up for the wedding. Everyone tried to convince Anthony that she had just gotten cold feet and ran off, but he knew better. He called the cops and they shut the Lodge down to look for her. They say that when they found her down there she was in the wedding gown, and she was soaking wet like she'd just taken a swim in the lake. One of the officers reported the floor being clean like it was just washed and the whole basement smelled like mildew. The Coroner is who ruled her death a drowning." Dana told the story in a hushed voice.

I could not help it. I cracked up. I laughed loud enough for the campers and Liam to look over in our direction, which of course ended our discussion as we were ushered to the others.

When we returned to High View we discovered the second floor door was boarded and nailed shut. Looking around, I noticed some of my stuff was missing from the common room. I glanced to Cat and without having to explain, she gave me a nod.

Lights out was called and we lay in our new beds waiting. Cat had lent me some sheets and a blanket since mine were upstairs. ruth be told, I didn't want any of the new stuff my grandparents had gotten me. They would be furious anyway. I just wanted Theadora my teddy bear, and Batty.

As Sumi made her rounds making sure we were asleep, we closed our eyes. It took all my willpower to keep my breaths even as I felt her standing over my bed staring at me. After about ten minutes, I felt a weight lifted from my body and knew she had moved on. A few minutes later, I heard the door to the bunk close with a soft thwack. I slowly opened an eye and quickly clamped a hand over my own mouth to smother my scream. On the support beam, directly across from my bed, were a set of almond shaped red glowing eyes.

I had never felt such a cold fear in my life. It took all my strength not to bolt out of the bunk. I had to keep telling myself that if I did, I would never see Babs or Gram again. I did not sleep that night. I just laid in bed trembling watching through barely opened eyes as the glowing red eyes that kept their vigil on me.

The next few weeks were a nightmare. It was all like one really long day. I could not remember the last time I had slept. I may have been thirteen, but I had slept with Theadora since I was like one. I just could not seem to fall asleep without her. And those glowing red eyes never left. They would appear after Sumi slipped out of our bunk every night adding to my stress and sleeplessness. With only two weeks left to my summer stay here, I knew something had to be done or I would never see Theadora again.

Cat and I, and even Dana, had grown close through all this. We stuck together like glue. None of us were ever alone. We quickly came up with a plan over breakfast and waited to put it into action. As we walked back from breakfast, Dana slipped into the art shack and grabbed a few cans of spray paint. I gave her questioning look, which she merely winked to.

Free Swim was where we were supposed to be after breakfast, but it was not mandatory. We chose not to go. In fact, the way we saw it, if we played our cards right Sumi would never even know we were not there.

"All right guys, time for free swim," Sumi called out.

The girls rushed out of the bunk in bathing suits with towels draped over a shoulder. Sumi looked at us and I was the one to speak. "We aren't going. We're going to go hang out in the canteen if Mike's okay with it."

Sumi gave me a definite glare. Her words were carefully and slowly spoken. "Fine. If he has a problem with you being there, find your own way to the pool." She slammed the door behind her as she left.

It had dawned on me that the eyes were never there during the day. Only at night, when it was dark. Since it was early in the day, the sun lit up High View like we actually had lights on. The three of us nodded to each other. It had been decided that Dana would keep watch, and Cat and I would find a way into the second floor where my stuff was.

We climbed the steps silently; the third step did not even creak. Cat produced a hammer with a nail remover on the back of the head and set to work tediously pulling the nails out of the board one at a time. Well, trying to. It proved to be a fruitless endeavor.

"We can go through the window. I doubt they nailed that shut. They'd never think of anyone trying to get in that way," I suggested.

Cat nodded and we quickly told Dana our plan and slipped out the back door. Cat kept watch from the back as I surveyed the stone work of the building. I began to quickly climb up the wall, the stones almost perfect foot and hand holds. I made it to the second floor window in no time, and just as I suspected, the window was untouched. I carefully took my right hand off the stone I was clutching and shimmied the window open just enough to hoist my body inside.

I found Theadora right where she had been dropped that morning, and picked her up with a smile. My smile was short-lived and rapidly slipped from my face as I saw, or rather did not see, Batty on my pillow anymore.

That's when I heard it. A bat scree quickly drawing closer. I ducked just in time to see Batty zip past me and slam into the wall above my bed. Still in the air, he shook his head and turned. That's when I saw the glowing red eyes on my poor little friend!

I tried to swallow the lump that formed in my throat to no avail, and as Batty dive bombed for-me again, I ran to the window and crawled out. I was sure I would fall to my death. In a last ditch effort, I grabbed the window sill and stopped my fall as my body slammed into High View's stone wall. I slipped my hand from the ledge to grasp a stone and slammed the window shut hard enough to crack the glass. My heart in my throat, I slid cautiously down the stones, landing in front of Cat. Even from the ground, we could clearly hear Batty's screes as he slammed himself over and over into the window I had escaped through.

"What the…" Cat started.

"We need to end this," I growled as I stormed off, ignoring all the aches and pains I was sure would blossom into a wonderful array of colorful bruises in a few hours.

We still had forty-five minutes before Free Swim would end, more than enough time to put the plan into action. We stormed up the gravel road and cut to the right. We knew the CiTs were out of Stone Lodge. They were not allowed to lounge around, and were all at their assigned classes. It truly was the ideal time to put the plan into motion.

We slipped soundly into Stone Lodge and looked around. While the outside gave the old ski lodge its name, the inside was coated in shellacked wood. A massive mantled fireplace sat as the main focus point in the common room with archways to other rooms branching off on either side. The last archway on the right held what we sought—the boarded and nailed up door to the basement. The boards had never been replaced. They looked old and warped. Cat did not even bother with the hammer. We each grabbed the top board and pulled. The whole mess that fell away from the door in about five minute's time. I took a deep breath, and felt Cat and Dana do the same beside me.

We exchanged glances, and then I opened the door.

The stench of mildew assailed us like a slap to the face. Fighting nausea, we began to descend the stairs, each of which creaked threateningly. We were forced to stop about three steps from the bottom. Water gently lapped at our ankles. I felt my toes squish in my sneakers. The liquid smelled putrid and I really did not want to spend more time down there than was necessary. I reached my hand back toward Dana, my gaze still on the dim basement. The only light was from the open doorway where we stood. My eyes fell of their own accord upon a yellowed wedding gown lying spread out on a table. I heard Cat suck in a breath and Dana swore under her breath. I knew then they were seeing what I saw. The dress began to fill out as if someone were wearing it. It took on curves of a women, yet there was no one wearing the dress that any of us could see. Then, the dress moved. The upper half lifted off the table.

As the arms of the wedding gown lifted, we heard a deep rumbling laugh before a massive set of those now all too familiar almond shaped, red, glowing eyes appeared in the darkest recesses of the basement.

"Dana now!" I yelled as I heard a few soft ting sounds, soft hissing sounds. Dana placed the now punctured cans of spray paint into my hands. Without a second thought, I started to back up as I fumbled in my pocket for my lighter.

We turned and ran for the door. I took a deep breath and hefted one of the hissing cans of spray paint. "Pretend it's a soft ball, pretend it's a softball," I chanted to myself as I lit the first can and hurled it into the opening of the basement. I lit the others much faster and threw them as we dived out of Stone Lodge.

We ran into the woods, heading down the hill toward the back of the Main House. My lungs felt as those they were on fire, my legs protesting the unjust torture I placed on them.

Dana, huffing along with us, managed to wheeze out. "You know, they aren't going to…"

A series of quick pops followed by a massive explosion stopped the last word from falling off Dana's lips. With renewed vigor, we used our reserves to duck and dodge the falling pieces of Stone Lodge before hurdling into the back door of the Main House, right into Mike's office.

"Well, hello girls. I see you've been having an adventurous morning." Mike said with a knowing smile. Though the rainbow of colors I was coated in probably clued him in to our activities.

Cat shrugged. "Just another day in Camp Linnenmyre."

No one knows what happened to Sumi. Mike never let on what actually happened to Stone Lodge. It was deemed an electrical fire. The last days of camp were okay. I continued to keep in touch with Dana and Catherine. Mike passed away not long after that incident, and Camp Linnenmyre found itself with yet another new owner. About a week after Mike passed, my mom handed me a package. My address was scrawled in Mike's familiar handwriting. Inside was a worn copy of the book *Atlas Shrugged* by Ayn Rand, and a silver key that looked like none I had ever seen before. A small note lay under it all. It read simply, "You'll know when it's time."

But that is a story for another time…

Love in Waiting
Margaret Egrot

Caro didn't need to draw back the curtains to know it was another wet day. From bed, she had heard the rain scolding the windows in bad tempered squalls and the wind moaning back just as angrily. So much for the summer solstice, she thought, and was briefly sorry for the intrepid sun worshippers she was sure would have made their way up to the stone circle by the lake, despite the storm and manifest lack of sun. After a promising April, and positively balmy May, the weather in June had taken a decidedly downward turn and was proving to be as dismal as she felt. Today was no different.

"What wouldn't I give to spend the day in bed?" she asked herself, rubbing her bare arms in the unseasonal early morning chill, before answering. "Nothing, nothing at all – not whilst there's still hope."

The rain was running over the gutters and turning the drive into a shallow river—her car was now standing in at least two inches of water. The drain was blocked again, she realised. She would have to get someone in but she didn't have time today, or any day soon, as far as she could see.

First, as every morning recently, she must pull on her tracksuit, wellington boots, and her old parka and take the two dogs out. Adverse elements never deterred Molly and Bella from their morning walk and she could hear them pawing imperiously at the kitchen door, and whimpering impatiently now that they had detected, from the creaking floorboards, that she was on the move. Could you both whimper and be imperious? Certainly, you could if you were a Molly or a Bella. She smiled a little at the thought— thank God the dogs still had the capacity to lift her spirits.

"OK you two, keep your fur on," she called out as she descended the stairs, grateful for their dogged determination to hold her to a regular morning routine. As she opened the kitchen door the usual morning mix of aromas from dog fur, dog breath, and raw canine energy greeted her. She caressed each proffered snout affectionately, before pushing them down and gathering up their leads and the back door key.

"Walkies!" she explained unnecessarily as the dogs shot out through the open door.

A blast of wind driven rain splashed over her face and shoulders as she too stepped outside, and she quickly pulled up her parka hood. Both dogs raced ahead, oblivious of the wetness all round them. She started to call them back to put them on their leads before they crossed the road, but then decided her neighbour wouldn't mind if she slipped through the hole in the fence, across his yard, and straight into the woods. It would be very muddy and the dogs would get filthy – but they were going to get thoroughly damp and dirty whichever way they went – both loved puddles, the deeper and muckier the better. And at least she could keep her hands relatively dry in her pockets if they ran free. Cheered a little by even such a small concession to comfort, she whistled to the dogs to follow her through the gap.

Soon all three were in the woods, with Molly and Bella racing ahead again and splashing with noisy abandon through all the puddles. She laughed—what was it with water and spaniels? No doubt that was why he, an enthusiastic hill walker in all weathers, said he particularly liked the breed, though she herself was generally happy with any dog that liked a bit of fuss and fun and was loving and loyal; pretty much anything that barked and wagged its tail in fact. But it was true; Bella and Molly were great companions. Without them, the house would feel too cold and empty.

"No, don't go there," she told herself, and dragged her mind onto more positive, practical, matters such as should she wash her hair when she got back to the house— or make it last another day. A wash, she decided, seeing as it was wet through already despite her hood. She whistled again for the dogs to follow her back to the house and, after a cursory sniff under some soggy weeds to show they would come at a time of their choosing, both bounded back to her side.

At the door, she waited whilst they shook themselves before letting them in and towelling them vigorously. Then she gave them a breakfast of meat and biscuits before going upstairs to remove her sodden clothes and jump under the shower.

The blast of hot water felt good on her chilled skin and she shook her head just like the dogs had done as she rinsed out the last of the shampoo. She blow-dried her hair quickly. It was well overdue a cut, she noticed, as the bottom layer stubbornly refused to curl under but, finding the time over the last few weeks had proved impossible, even finding time (and motivation) to eat properly was a challenge.

With her hair more or less respectable, she turned her attention to her clothes. It had never taken her long to dress. By habit she put on more or less the same outfit each morning: a cream silk blouse, slim-line black trousers, a light gray jacket, black shoes—heels not too high as they needed to be comfortable enough to pound the hospital corridors; good quality, but stylish—as she felt he had always appreciated. She looked at herself in the mirror and smiled ruefully. No need to worry about putting on weight. These days the pounds seemed to be dropping off her and she could, she experimented briefly, now put both hands inside her waistband and push down almost half way to her elbow. Despite this, she didn't think she could face breakfast.

She paid careful attention to her make-up, skilfully masking the bags under her eyes and adding eyeliner to conceal the evidence of sleepless nights. Was this being silly at her age? Was he worth all the tossing and turning? She knew the answer. Then she added a touch of blusher to both cheeks and applied a cheerful red lipstick to her lips. She was almost pleased with the result and smiled back at her reflection. Maybe today would be the day when he would sit up and take notice of her – well show some awareness of her existence anyway. Finally, she added a splash of perfume to her wrists and down her cleavage. Flower By Kenzo, eau de parfum—because he had once mentioned in passing how he liked the light flowery smell. She hadn't normally worn scent, except to go out in the evening; now she wore it every day.

She paused in the kitchen, but still couldn't summon up any appetite for breakfast. She would get a coffee once she got to the hospital and maybe some food later. She gave the dogs a farewell pat. They licked her hand but didn't otherwise clamour for her attention. They knew the routine: she would be back later, maybe much later, but she had arranged with a neighbour to come in and take them out during the day; and come in again later to give them their evening meal. She picked up her briefcase, carefully packed the night before, and said goodbye to each dog. She knew the hopeful looks in their eyes was more likely to be an attempt to persuade her to take them with her, wherever she was going, but she wanted to read from their expressions that they were wishing her well. Maybe today...

She paddled gingerly to the car, fired up the engine and pulled out of the drive. This was an easy manoeuvre when there was just just one car and, setting the wipers on fast, she was soon inching her way up the flooded lane. She paused at the corner to let a huddle of bedraggled druids cross in front of her, but once on the dual carriageway that would take her straight to the hospital, she put her foot down and completed the journey in good time.

The rain was easing a little as Caro pulled into the hospital car park. She cursed, as usual, the recent egalitarian policy change that meant that everyone—senior consultants, junior nurses, even hospital visitors, had to take potluck on when and where they could park—and then pay a hefty fee each day for the privilege. But the sun, at least metaphorically, was shining on her endeavours that morning, and she quickly found a parking bay. She jumped out of the car, took her briefcase from the passenger seat, and half jogged-half sprinted to the entrance without bothering to put her umbrella up.

As usual when she reached the hospital, she felt a new surge of energy and optimism for what the day might bring, and maintained her brisk pace. The regular staff on reception acknowledged her as she sped past them and along the corridor, exchanging the usual

"Morning, how are you?"

"Fine thanks. And you?"

Funny isn't it, she thought, how even after all this time, none of us really knows anything about each other. Though probably, she thought further, the two women on reception knew a lot more about her than she did about them.

"That's Dr. Niles. You know, the one who..."

"Oh yes, I wonder if he..."

"I can't see it happening..."

"Ah well, she lives in hope, maybe that's all she can do."

"Poor thing, she must be getting desperate by now."

Was it so bloody obvious? She hoped not. She hoped they had better things to gossip about.

Finally, she was at the right ward. It was a small cubicle really, rather than a ward, containing just one bed, a clutter of medical equipment, and a little window overlooking rear car park. She looked through the porthole shaped window in the door and tapped to attract the attention of the nurse who was busy at the small sink under the window. The nurse looked up, smiled, and beckoned her in. Caro's eyes went straight to the middle-aged man lying on the bed, linked by numerous tubes to a bank of monitors.

"Any change, Eileen?"

"No, Dr. Niles, I'm afraid not."

"Well no-one said it would be any time soon."

"True. God moves in a mysterious way. Sometimes very mysterious to us mere mortals."

Normally Caro hated any religious talk, especially in a hospital setting, but she liked and trusted Eileen, and found her soft Irish brogue soothing. Her simple devoutness, always delivered with a gentle smile, had been strangely comforting over the past few weeks. She smiled back as brightly as she could and the nurse touched her arm.

"Time," repeated Caro. "Fortunately the university has told me again to take all the time I want; and student lectures will be finishing soon."

"Meanwhile we must all practice patience, and I'll keep praying," said Eileen as she wrote something on the clipboard on the wall by the sink. "I've just checked everything and there's no change. Now, you just sit down and make yourself comfortable and I'll go and get you a coffee. Maybe a croissant too, you need to keep your energy up."

"Both would be lovely, thank you. Mustn't get too gaunt–he's always liked a few curves."

Caro settled herself down as the nurse left and only then gave her full attention to her husband.

"How are you today, my love?" she started.

"Bella and Molly send their love, and big fat slobbery licks as usual. And today, a special wet and chilly shake of rain and mud from their walk." Her husband lay impassive; the monitors blinked steadily, the machinery clicked rhythmically. She ploughed on.

"Yes, it's another rainy day. Heading for the wettest June in decades, they say. Not even any let up for the summer solstice. Those poor druids! They were soaked through by the time they finished chanting over the lake. I saw some of them heading back home. I didn't go as far as the stone circle with the dogs today. Way too wet!

"Do you remember, Ian, all the sunny picnics we've had out by the lake on midsummer night? And when we watched the sun go down over the top of the forest? Well we're not missing anything if we pass on that trip today!

"The drain's blocked again. I'll have to get a man in if you don't buck up and get home soon."

Her voice faltered. She was struggling already with the one sided conversation whilst her husband lay on his bed, as unresponsive as the day before, and the days before that. She leaned a little closer and touched the small part of his nearest hand that wasn't linked to a monitor.

"You stupid, stupid man," she said softly, as she did every day when the nurse was out of the room. "Why, did you have to rush out that evening? I didn't mind that you'd forgotten to buy flowers. I told you that. Twenty-seven years of marriage; not a special date, even for us. You could have bought me a bunch the next morning if you had to. But you, you romantic old fool, you just had to drive off to the florist there and then. And now look!"

She kissed his forehead and squeezed his fingers, before loosening her grip to rummage in her briefcase. First she pulled out a clean pair of pyjamas, then a fresh tube of cream for bed sores, which she put on the bedside cupboard, and then a book. A large, battered paperback.

"Here we go again," she said brightly. "Ulysses. Ghastly old Joyce. But you always said you wanted to get round to reading him when you had the time. And now you've got the time—all the time in the world. So, I'm going to keep reading until you wake up. And if you haven't by the time I come to the end—why I'll just start reading it all over again. And again—until you can't stand it anymore, and just have to come round so as to shut me up. We're going to get to grips with this wordy old leprechaun's work if it kills us. Except it won't my love, because we're going to get through this together, as we've done everything else for the past twenty-seven years. So, listen up my boy! Now, where were we?"

She opened the book where she had left the bookmark the evening before and, leaning close to him so that he could catch the perfume on her skin, she started to read:

"Chapter eighteen. Wait, my love, and I'll be with you..."

She read slowly, her voice little more than a gentle murmur. The book lay on her lap and she turned each page with her right hand and stroked her husband's fingers with her left.

The nurse seemed to be taking a long time bringing her coffee and as turned the next page she paused to clear her throat. At the same time she felt, maybe just sensed, a slight movement under her left hand. Or did she? She looked across to the bed quickly.

Ian was just as he had been before. Mute, impassive. It had just been wishful thinking. Like the last time, and the five times before that. Trust me, she thought sadly, to keep a tally of these false dawns. She shifted herself slightly to avoid a streak of watery sunshine that was now bravely showing itself through the small window and was streaming directly into her eyes.

She looked back down at the book. It was no use rushing things. It was pointless fooling herself. But one day there had to be a change. Had to! That was why she came every morning and stayed until late into the evening. Why all her teaching and research was on hold. Why friends and family were ignored. So she must keep hoping, and trying. She leant her head closer to her husband's and almost breathed into his ear.

"Ian, dear. Do you want me to keep on reading?"

It was unmistakeable this time. A definite, if momentary, pressure on her fingers. She didn't dare look down at her hand, but she felt tears pricking at her eyes, and joy such as she'd never experienced before. She had to work hard to resist the urge to throw herself on the bed and hug him to her. Instead, she sat quite still facing the window, fingers interlaced with those of her husband, and only looked round as the door clicked open.

"My, I'm sorry, Dr. Niles, to be so long, but look I've managed to get you an almond croissant fresh baked from the kitchens," Eileen bustled in, pleased with her small success with the new chef, but then noticed Caro's face.

"Why, whatever is the matter, you've gone quite white. Has something awful happened whilst I was out?"

Eileen looked quickly from Caro to her patient and, as he seemed to be just as she'd left him, she looked back at Caro and noticed fresh tears rolling unhindered down her cheeks.

"He squeezed my hand. Really he did."

Eileen put the coffee and plate down carefully. Despite her prayers and her faith, she had learnt never to be too optimistic in this job. She was used to her patient's families detecting non-existent signs of renewed life. And used, as well, to sitting with the doctor as they broke it gently to so many relatives that there really was no more room for hope. But she had come to see Dr. Niles as a level headed kind of lady, even if a little odd wanting to read that Joyce fellow's ramblings to her husband all day long. Eileen had been born and brought up in Dublin before emigrating as a young woman, but she'd never seen the point of Ulysses, or any other piece of high faulting nonsense by that so called national treasure.

She put a hand on Caro's shoulder, and Caro looked up at her, eyes shining through the tears:

"Wouldn't it be lovely, Eileen, if today of all days

he came to? Mid-summer's day and, look, a brave new sun shining in on him through the window."

"Now, Dr. Niles, don't be building up your hopes." Eileen replied cautiously.

"I'm not. Believe me he really did squeeze my hand. Maybe he won't do it again today. Maybe he's too tired now. But maybe he will. Just humour me and watch our hands."

She turned from the nurse and leant towards her husband. Speaking slowly and clearly right by his ear, her hand intertwined with his, she repeated:

"Ian, dear, do you want me to continue reading?"

Despite her scepticism, Eileen watched closely. Her eyes widened, her mouth fell open. Then she crossed herself.

"Holy Mary, Mother of God!" Was all she said before running out of into the corridor. Caro smiled as she heard the nurse's voice fade away as she reached the doctors' office. She turned back to the bed. Soon there would be a large cluster of medics and nurses in the little room but, for a few precious moments, it was just her and Ian.

"I don't believe in miracles," she told her husband. "I can't stand Joyce. I'm sorry the solstice has been a complete wash out for the druids. I'm worried about the blocked drain back home. My hair's a mess and I look like an anorexic scarecrow. But speaking personally, my love, today has been worth all the worry and waiting. Today is the best day of my life."

Slowly, weakly, perceptible only to her, Ian squeezed her fingers again, as if in agreement. His lips moved fractionally for the first time, and she leant leaned in so that her ear was almost on his mouth. She wasn't sure, but she thought she heard him whisper one word:

"Caro."

The Bully
Charmaine Pauls

Tricea stirred sweetener into her Earl Gray tea. "Max is a little pest. Everyone knows."

"I don't know, Tricea." Cordette looked at the children jumping over foam rubber forms in the obstacle playpen. "Bennie hasn't said anything. Neither have any of the other moms."

"Are you saying my Johnny is a liar?"

"Of course not. I'm just saying…" Cordette shrugged.

Tricea's pinky tilted when she lifted her cup. "You should be careful with your Amy," she said to Mildred, "her being new in school. I'm telling you, Max is a bully."

Deloris broke a croissant in half. "Come here, Tommie!" She waved the piece at a red-haired boy. "It happens so early these days. Can you imagine? Not even five years old and we already have to deal with bullies. Tommie! Come here. Now!" She lowered her hand when Tommie ignored her, blushing slightly. "Oh well, he's eaten so much this morning."

"Tricea," Gretha finished her Coke with a slurp of the straw, "be careful not to label the poor kid before he's even started Grade One."

"I thought Max and Johnny were friends?" Gretha asked. She chewed on her straw, regarding Tricea from the rim of her glass.

"Exactly. Max manipulates Johnny. He's not allowed to play with anyone else. It's as if Max claims exclusivity on Johnny. Have you ever heard of anything so absurd?"

"Isn't that normal behavior at this age?" Gretha said.

"Normal?" Tricea laughed. "What do you say, Mildred?"

"I understand Tricea's concern."

"But what's your opinion of Max?" Tricea said.

Mildred fumbled with a packet of sugar. "Maybe we should speak to the principal."

Gretha snorted. "He's too busy for pre-school squabbles. Just let the kids fight it out among themselves."

"Can't you just talk to Max's mom, Tricea?" Deloris said.

Gretha checked her mobile phone. "Got to go." She retrieved her handbag and sighed. "Homework. At this tender age. Freddie—" she projected her voice to carry across the noisy room to the play area—"say goodbye to your friends." She fetched a blond boy from the pile of kids and dragged him to the cashier where she paid.

"Yes, it's getting late." Mildred pushed her chair back.

"You must bring Amy over to the house for a play date," Tricea said. "I'll call you."

"Thank you. That's so kind."

Cordette picked up the bill and scrunched up her eyes as she studied it. When Tricea snatched the piece of paper from her hand, Cordette slowly lowered her fingers, her lips pursed.

"I'll get this one," Tricea said. "You get the next."

The tightness of Cordette's jaw visible relaxed. "Are you sure they didn't overcharge us?"

"It's fine," Tricea said, barely glancing at the slip."Remember, Gretha has paid for her part. Check that they don't double charge you."

"Come, Johnny dear," Tricea called. "Mommy's going to be late for her date."

For a few minutes there was a good deal of protesting and crying as the women collected their children to leave the playroom of the café.

***

Mildred left Amy in front of the television while she threw a hasty dinner of pasta and ham together. A squeal from Amy made her lift her head. Through the kitchen window she saw Michael's car pulling into the driveway. She watched Amy run outside to be picked up and swirled around in Michael's arms. Father and daughter came into the kitchen, hand in hand, Michael laughing and Amy skipping.

Michael kissed Mildred on the cheek. "Hi, Pumpkin. How was your day?"

Mildred gave the pasta a stir and turned the gas down. "So-so."

"Didn't Amy have a play date at the café today? It must have been good to socialize with the other moms."

Mildred stepped around her husband to set the table. "It was all right."

"What's wrong?" Michael sat down at the kitchen table and pulled Amy into his lap.

"I just feel guilty, that's all. I should have left much earlier. But Tricea wouldn't let me. I couldn't get away."

Michael pushed the knife around on the placemat. "Why would you feel guilty?"

"It's already past Amy's bedtime." She turned the gas off and drained the pasta. "She'll be tired for school tomorrow. I hate disrupting her schedule."

Michael patted Amy's head. "She doesn't look tired. And you had fun, right? It doesn't happen every day. Just enjoy the opportunity when it comes along. You did have fun, right?"

Mildred carried the pot to the table and dumped it on a cork mat on the far side, out of Amy's reach.

"Yes. Of course." She replaced the knife in its proper position and sat down. "Amy, go wash your hands. Hurry up. Mommy's really late tonight, okay?"

When Amy ran off to the bathroom, Michael said, "Don't rush her. She doesn't have a concept of time. You'll raise her to be stressed."

Mildred pursed her lips and dipped the serving spoon into the pot. "Pasta?" She dropped it onto Michael plate before he replied. "Sorry. I didn't have time to cook."

Amy came back into the kitchen, taking her usual place next to Mildred. "I don't like this pasta, Mommy."

"Well, that's all there is tonight. I haven't been to the shop, so I don't have spirals." Mildred put a serving on

Amy's plate. "Have some ham with it. I promise to cook meatballs with spaghetti tomorrow." She motioned to Michael to eat. "Sorry."

"It's fine, Pumpkin. I don't mind, as long as you had fun. Maybe you should rather cook for lunch, and serve Amy a light dinner. That will give you ample time to cook in the morning. You can save me a plate for dinner." When Mildred shot him a look, he lifted an eyebrow. "I'm only making a practical suggestion. When Amy gets older there will be afternoon sports and other activities, I imagine, and anyway, it's healthier for her to have a decent lunch and a small dinner."

Mildred pushed her chair back and stomped to the kitchen sink.

Michael put his fork down. "What?" He raised his hands. "What did I say now?"

She resisted the urge to pick a glass from the drip tray and to throw it against the wall.

"Come back to the table, Mildred. Set an example for Amy."

Mildred stood for another few seconds, taking deep breaths, before turning to the pantry and carrying the salt to the table. She sat down.

"Are you not having dinner?" Michael said.

"I had cake at the café, which I didn't want, but since everyone had, I felt obliged to. Now it's going to take a week to lose the weight."

Michael started eating again. She looked away.

"Oh, what? What did I say?" he said.

She opened her mouth and shut it again, and then, despite her intentions, she said, "I don't like the way you assume that I'm never going back to work, that I'm always going to be here to drive Amy around and to cook our meals."

Michael stared at his plate, frowning. He chewed for a long time. When he spoke again, it was with a low voice. "I

42

thought this is what you wanted, to be at home for Amy."

"This is what *you* wanted. I'm sick to death of staying at home. I'm bored. Don't you see what it's doing to me?"

Michael's head shot up. "Hush, Pumpkin. Not now." He glanced at Amy. "We'll talk about this later, in bed."

"We shouldn't talk in bed. It always leads to a fight. That's why we don't…"

"We'll talk when Amy is in bed."

"All the other women are wealthy. They have maids and do nothing all day. I can't simply go out when I want to. I have to clean and cook. I can't afford to sit in the hair salon or in the nail bar, or have long lunches like them. They think we're like them, just because we live in this neighborhood, but we're not!"

"I don't understand why you're getting so upset. I thought we were going to make a new start here. Please. If needed, we'll find you a new doctor and you can go back on your medication." He paused. A look of exasperation came over his face. "You have all the reason in the world to be happy."

"I don't fit in! Don't you see?" She looked away so that Amy wouldn't notice the tears in her eyes.

"What's wrong, Mommy?"

Michael dropped his fork in his plate. "You've upset her. Are you happy now?" He wiped his mouth on a napkin and threw it down. "Come, Amy. Daddy will put you to bed. Mommy's got a headache."

Mildred watched as Michael picked Amy up and carried her from the kitchen, as if she had to be removed from a contaminated room.

She looked at the window, but her eyes were focused on the blurry view inside herself.

***

Leaving Johnny's dinner and bath to Jenny, her child minder, Tricea could get ready for their dinner appointment. She sat on the stool in the dressing room applying the finishing touches to her makeup when her husband walked in.

Albert regarded her with approval. "You look gorgeous, as always. Sorry I'm late." He bent down to kiss her.

"Careful, my lipstick will smudge. Are you changing?"

He looked down at his day suit. "Should I?"

She sighed, studying herself in the mirror. "I don't know. I'm too tired to think for both of us."

"Why so tired?" Albert stepped around her to his side of the room and removed his tie. "Have you been to the gym?"

She slipped on her earrings. "I had a very tiring afternoon with Johnny's friends and their moms. I barely had time to get ready. It was such a rush. Can you pour me a glass of wine before the driver gets here?"

Albert flipped through his ties. "I'll ask Jenny to bring you one. Could do with a drink myself."

She picked up her evening bag and got to her feet. "Forget it. I'll get the drinks. I don't want Jenny to think we're alcoholics."

Albert lifted a shirt from the shelf and held it up with the tie. "Do these go together?"

Tricea barely glanced at him on her way to the door. "Whatever. You have good dress sense. I'm not your mother, for goodness sake."

"Why so prickly tonight? Is it the dinner?"

"No, I know how important these clients are. I didn't want to bring it up until later, but since you asked, I'm worried about Johnny."

"Why?" Albert started to unbutton his shirt. "What happened?"

"Max bullies him. I spoke to the other moms and they agree that Max is a terror. You wonder what kind of parents he's got."

"Johnny is a boy." He pulled on the clean shirt. "He'll

sort himself out."

"Will you watch him take a hammering without doing anything? Do you know how damaging it is for a child's self-esteem? He may never develop assertiveness."

"Let's face it," Albert said, turning to the mirror to tie his tie, "Johnny is a bit of a coward. Especially when it comes to fighting back. A little pushing and shoving may be good for him. He has to learn how to defend himself."

"That's just like you. You want him to be one hundred percent man, don't you? I suppose if he grows up not liking football or beer you'll find fault with that too. What if he wants to learn to play the piano?"

He turned and put his arms around her waist. "Stop bickering." He kissed her neck. "You look much too good for a fight."

The doorbell rang. She pulled away. "The car is here. Now look, I didn't even have time for my glass of wine."

Albert picked up his jacket and escorted her to the door, his hand on the small of her back. "I'll order you a bottle, as soon as we get there."

They stopped in Johnny's room to kiss him goodnight. He was already asleep.

***

Gretha sat on the toilet seat, drinking beer straight from the bottle. Henry lay in the bath, only his head and hands visible above the foam. His slender fingers rested on the stem of his wineglass.

"Why do you still see them if they irritate you so?" he said.

Gretha propped her foot on the edge of the bath. "Because I have to. Because our kids are friends."

"But why not drop Freddie off and fetch him after the play date?"

"Because a coffee play date doesn't work like that. They play. We drink coffee. Besides, if I'm not there, I won't know what they say about me behind my back. Or about Freddie."

Henry closed his eyes and laid his head back. "You women."

"Oh, come on, Babes, you're more like a woman than any one of us."

He smiled. "Don't pick on me because I'm a sensitive artist."

"Since you are a stay-at-home artist, you could have at least bathed Freddie before falling into the bubbles yourself." She rubbed her neck. "I had a tough day at the office. I can't believe I spent my once-a-month afternoon off on a play date."

"I was covered in paint."

"As every day." She closed one eye and peeped into the neck of the bottle. "I hate those stupid cows. Deloris has no backbone, Cordette is a parasite and Mildred has no opinion of her own. Tricea thinks she owns everyone."

He sat up and trailed his hand over her arm. "Stop thinking about those awful cows, and get into the bath with me."

She slapped at his hand, laughing. "I have to bathe Freddie," but even as she said it, she was already unbuttoning her shirt.

The bathroom door opened and Freddie ran inside. Giggling, he bent over the bath, scooped up a hand full of foam and deposited it on Henry's head. Henry caught Freddie's arm and rewarded him with a bubble bath beard, inviting excited yells. Gretha watched them silently. She left the bottle on the floor, got up and walked to the door. Just before closing it, she saw Henry pull Freddie into the bath, clothes and all, making a terrible mess. They were too absorbed in each other to notice her exit.

***

The sounds of a referee blowing a whistle and a commentator's excited voice filled the lounge. Cordette stood in front of her husband, blocking the television. Her hands were balled at her sides. She clutched a spatula in one.

"Pieter, I am talking to you! You didn't hear a word I said."

He craned his neck. "Move away, will you!"

She slapped him with the spatula on the knee.

"Hey! What the hell was that for?"

"Pieter Mulder, it's a video recording of the rugby match for crying out loud! How many times have you watched it already?"

"What?" He shrugged. "I don't criticize you for watching your soapies. For God's sake..."

"Don't roll your eyes at me! I said, you didn't hear a word I said."

"I did." He leaned across the armrest of his Lazy Boy and took another beer from the six-pack. "You said Johnny got beaten up by a kid from school. Serves him right, the spoilt brat."

"Pieter!" Cordette's shoulders dropped. "Really. Sometimes I don't know why I try to involve you at all."

He cracked open the beer and mumbled through slurping the foam boiling over the opening, "Neither ... damn-well I."

"What did you say?"

"Nothing."

She narrowed her eyes. "I heard that."

He sighed. "So, what happened to Johnny?"

"That's the point. Nothing. Maybe he got one smack. Which he asked for, mind you. Tricea is totally overreacting. Just because they've got money doesn't mean she can shunt everyone around, or beat up the other moms because their kids take a stance against Johnny. He's so small, and so short, and yet he acts like he's king. I'm sure that's the way they treat him at home. I wonder what went wrong genetically? I mean, Albert is not bad looking, or *that* short. And all that dark hair... I bet you he's going to

47

grow hair on his back one day. I wonder if Albert has hair on his back? I don't like what Tricea is doing."

"Why get involved? It's not your fight."

"Next thing you know she'll declare war against Bennie. I'm trying to ignore it, but it's really grinding on my nerves."

"Try harder." He burped.

"Did you take the dog for a walk?" She headed back toward the kitchen.

"Nope."

She turned at the door. "Then I guess that means you haven't helped Bennie with his reading, have you?"

He picked up the remote and pushed the rewind button. "Let him be. He's young. Let him play. Children his age should be playing outside, not reading."

"He'll fall behind the others in his class if he doesn't keep up with his homework, and we both know he has a problem."

The sliding door slammed. Bennie stood in the lounge, his shoes muddy and his shirt wet. "I'm hungry."

Cordette looked at the floor Bennie was soiling. "I'm busy cooking dinner. Why are you wet? I told you it's forbidden to play with the hosepipe." She turned to Pieter. "Do something. I'm not an octopus. I only have two hands."

Pieter glanced in Bennie's direction before his eyes fixed on the screen again. "Bennie, listen to your mother. Take off your shoes and go run your bath."

"Oh, just forget it." Cordette threw the spatula on the nearby table. "I'll do it myself, even if I'm not the one who sits at home without a job drinking beer all day. Oh no, I work, I cook, I clean, but that's okay. Why don't I just take care of everything?" She walked to Bennie and grabbed his arm. "Come." She pulled him down the hallway. "And if your dinner is burned," she yelled back at her husband, "don't come crying to me."

**

Tommie fell asleep in the car on the way to the shelter where Deloris took care of the soup kitchen on Thursday evenings. She carried him inside. He woke up when they entered the cold kitchen and started crying.

"Where have you been?" Richard asked, looking up from a heap of peeled potatoes.

"Play date." She kissed her husband on the cheek, squashing Tommie between them. His crying turned to wailing.

"We have a responsibility here, Deloris. If you can't commit, then don't agree to do it."

She lowered Tommie onto a chair. He kicked at her shin. "Tommie! Relax, Richard. We're only thirty minutes late."

"Thirty-seven minutes."

Deloris knelt in front of Tommy. "What's wrong, baby?"

"Don't pamper him. What he needs is a good hiding."

Deloris took a piece of bread from the table and gave it to Tommie. It went flying through the air.

"Talking of which," Deloris said, "Tricea said Max hits Johnny."

"Who's Max?"

"Max," Deloris insisted, "from their class."

"Cut up those carrots, will you? The water is nearly boiling."

Deloris tied an apron around her waist. "I don't know if I agree."

Richard removed his glasses and cleaned them with the corner of his sweatshirt. "With what? Tommie, stop crying!"

"Don't yell at him, Richard. It's not his fault. He's tired."

"Then do something. I can't stand his screaming."

Deloris placed a carrot on the cutting board. "I don't

know if Johnny is so innocent. Maybe he is at fault, too. There are always two sides to a story."

"If you don't do something with Tommie, I'm going to smack him."

"He should be at home, in bed."

"So why didn't you come earlier?"

"I told you. We had a play date. It's only once a month. Tommie looks forward to it."

"Really, Deloris, sometimes I don't understand your priorities."

A gray-haired woman came through the door. She looked at Tommie. "No, no, don't cry, dear. Want to come with Auntie May?"

"Go away!" Tommie yelled.

"Oh, Tommie," Deloris said, "don't be rude to old people."

"I'm not old," the woman said.

"I'm not saying that. I'm teaching him respect for his elders."

The woman snorted and walked off.

"I don't know why I'm still doing this," Deloris said. "Nobody is ever thankful. All they do is complain. The soup is too cold, the soup is too hot, not enough salt, not enough meat, they're tired of eating soup…"

Richard carried the potatoes to two big pots on the stove and threw them into the boiling water. "Then why don't you go home, Deloris?" He glared at her, his glasses pinched on the bridge of his nose by his frown.

She turned her back on him. "Maybe I will." But she carried on chopping carrots, while Tommie whined.

***

There wasn't a single space to park. Mildred swore as she drove around the school twice.

She turned in her seat. "I told you to hurry up, Amy. Now look. We're going to be late."

She sighed and double-parked in front of the

50

entrance as the bell rang.

"Unbuckle your seatbelt, Amy. Quickly."

Mildred jumped from the car and ran around the back to get Amy's school bag from the boot. Halfway to the gate, she realized that Amy was still in the car. She rushed back and flung the door open.

"Amy! What now?"

"I can't get the belt to open, Mommy."

"Arg!" Mildred battled with the seatbelt, and finally managed to free her. "Run, Amy!" she cried as they both made for the gate.

Mildred's advance was once more delayed when she remembered that she hadn't locked the car. She swore again, running back to push the remote button.

When she got to the gate, breathless, Amy had already gone through without saying goodbye. Mildred stood on the spot, defeated and miserable. There was no point in trying to sneak through, as the guard was already eyeing her.

He stepped up. "Sorry, no parents through the gates after the bell."

"I know that," she bit out.

Someone called her name. She saw Tricea and the usual group standing under the big tree. Tricea waved.

Mildred looked in Amy's direction one last time, hoping that she would turn and wave. When Amy disappeared through her classroom door without a backward glance, Mildred walked to the women gathered on the lawn.

"Hey, everyone. Gosh. Late again. Mornings. Such a rush."

"Don't you get up early?" Tricea said. "I've already been to the gym."

"I don't have a maid to dress and feed Amy in the morning."

"Why don't you get one?"

Mildred pushed her hands into her coat pockets. "I'll get round to it."

"I don't have one," Gretha said. "Just can't stand someone around me all day. Someone who's not family, I mean."

"But you've got Henry," Cordette said, "and he does a lot around the house."

"I have to get to work." Gretha jingled her car keys. "Enjoy your life of leisure."

Tricea had taken sunblock from her bag, which she was dabbing on her face. "Shall we go for a coffee?"

"All right," Deloris said. She looked at Mildred.

"Can't really," Mildred said meekly. "I've got to get the washing in the machine."

Tricea slipped her hand through Mildred's arm. "Oh, come on, it can wait. Let's grab a quick one."

Mildred pulled her arm free. "I'm sorry." She looked away. "I have to go now."

Mildred ran back to her car. She was about to turn the key in the ignition when she noticed the parking fine stuck in her windscreen wiper. She sat staring at it for several seconds. A sob broke from her throat. She started the car and drove around the block, out of sight, where she had to pull over onto the curb. It took ten minutes before she could see enough to continue driving.

Mildred didn't stop crying until the washing was on the line. While vacuuming, a sense of guilt attacked her. What if Tricea didn't want to be friends with her after her morning's performance? Maybe she really could have let the house go unattended. Maybe it would have been fun, a coffee with Tricea. She had no friends as it was. She switched the vacuum cleaner on and off twice, and finally she made up her mind and went for a shower. She pulled on a floral dress and dried her curly hair straight. The daunting task took no less than an hour. Finally, she stepped back from the mirror, undecided. She plucked the dress over her head and changed into jeans and a wool sweater, and then she swapped the sweater for a polo neck jersey. She had to brush her hair again. She called Tricea.

"It's Mildred," she said when Tricea answered.

"Oh, hi."

"I'm sorry about this morning," she recited. "I had so much to do at home. Anyway, I've done the washing," she laughed self-consciously, "so we can go now, if you want."

"I had coffee with a few girls from my charity this morning who I wanted to introduce you to. I'm at the spa now. Albert gave me a voucher for the day. Won't be out until five, maybe six."

Mildred forced herself to sound bright. "Maybe we can go tomorrow?"

"Tomorrow? I've got this fundraising thing at the club."

"No matter. Let me know, then."

"Sure. See you at school."

Even before Tricea had hung up, she was already talking to someone else in the background.

Mildred looked at the phone. It was almost time to fetch Amy, and she hadn't cooked lunch. Mildred threw the phone against the wall, and slid to the floor. She hid her face in her hands and started sobbing again.

***

The vegetable market was cold. Deloris had to run to keep up with Henry as he walked through the aisles.

"We have to hurry," he said, "or all the best produce will be gone."

"Sorry I was so late to pick you up this morning," she said. Henry stopped at a fruit vendor to inspect the oranges. "I just couldn't say no to Tricea when she suggested having a coffee."

"Why not?"

"I have a hard time saying no."

"You should learn to."

53

"Why the rush, anyway?"

"I'm working on something."

"What?"

He lifted a bunch of carrots by their green stalks. "Right now, I'm working on vegetables."

"I thought you did portraits."

"Mmm. Look," he pointed at a bunch of grapes, "this looks yum."

"Richard would have a fit. Those are imported."

Henry threw two packets in his pull cart. "Come. Let's be quick."

"Why? The market doesn't close until twelve."

"I'm inspired, suddenly."

Deloris watched Henry gather vegetables and fruit from every stall they passed.

"Are you really going to use all of that in a week?" she said.

"Don't know. I'll see which recipes tickle my fancy."

"Cordette should pay more attention to Bennie's diet. He's already as round as Pieter."

"That's because they don't do any exercise. How's the new mom?"

"Mildred? Don't know. She doesn't say much."

"I'm done. Shall we go?"

Deloris looked at her empty basket. "I promised Richard I'd get the veggies for next week's soup kitchen."

"You carry on shopping. I'll catch a taxi home."

Before Deloris could answer, Henry disappeared down the rows of pineapples and artichokes.

***

Shortly after Mildred had arrived at the school gate, Deloris rushed up to her.

"Hi, Mildred. Your hair looks nice. Been to the hairdresser?"

"Thanks. No. I just dried it properly for a change."

"Are you okay? We were worried about you this

morning."

"Yes, of course. The move hasn't been easy. I'm just a bit stressed, that's all. I have so much to do."

"I know what you mean. Where do the hours of the day go, right? Anyway," she moved forward with the rest of the parents pushing through the gates, "you can be glad you didn't go."

"Really?"

"Tricea went on and on about Cinthea. I just don't know if it's right."

"Who's Cinthea?"

"You know, Max's mom. She's still on about that. You mustn't pay too much attention to Tricea. She can exaggerate a bit. Oh, look. No. Don't look now. There she is. Max's mom. In front of the class."

Mildred saw a short woman with a spiky-haired boy in hand. "Do you know her?"

"Not really." Deloris shrugged. "We've said hi. But that's about it."

When the dark-haired woman neared them, she looked up and smiled. "Hello, Deloris."

"Hi, Cinthea. This is Mildred, Amy's mom."

"Hi Mildred," Cinthea extended her hand. "Amy is such a pretty thing. Is she your only child?"

Mildred cleared her throat. "For now."

"Well, nice to meet you."

Mildred watched Cinthea and Max walk off. "She seems nice."

"Who knows these days? Oh, look, there's my Tommie."

Tommie ran down the corridor, almost knocking Deloris over.

"Slowly, Tommie. Say hi to Auntie Mildred." Tommie ignored them both. Deloris smiled uncomfortably. "Such a long day for the kids. They get so tired."

"I can imagine."

"Tricea is calling a meeting with the moms of the class, minus Cinthea, to talk about Max."

"That doesn't seem right."

"She doesn't want to say anything to Cinthea unless the other moms feel the same way about Max. That does sound kind of fair, doesn't it?"

"I suppose."

Tommie plucked at Deloris' coat. "I want to go now. Stop talking. I want to go home."

"Run along and get Amy," Deloris said, waving as she made her way to the exit.

Mildred rushed to the classroom. Amy was the last one left. Mildred bent down to hug her. When Amy didn't respond, Mildred said, "Aren't you happy to see me?"

Amy shrugged. "Sure. Is it Friday? Is it true that there is no school tomorrow?"

"Yes. You can sleep in." She took Amy's school bag. "Are you glad?"

"No! I never want to come back to this school."

"Why not?"

"I hate it here."

"But Amy! Why?"

"I'm always last to come and late to go."

"Come on," Mildred said.

"Did you make meatballs and spaghetti, Mommy?"

"I didn't have time, Amy. We'll have a sandwich. I promise I'll cook tonight."

"You always make promises but you don't keep them." Amy crossed her arms. "I will never believe you, ever again!" She started crying.

Mildred turned and started walking. She didn't glance back to see if Amy was following. She simply kept going. She almost bumped into an attractive man with green eyes of such a light color they were disturbing to look at.

"You're Amy's mom, right?"

"Yes?"

"I'm Henry, Freddie's dad. Gretha told me so much about you. I've seen you pick up Amy a couple of times, but I've never had a chance to introduce myself."

"Nice to meet you." Henry didn't say anything in response, and when the silence stretched, Mildred said, "Gretha said you're an artist."

"A struggling artist."

She looked around. "Where's Freddie?"

He pointed at the playground. "Over there. I always let him play a bit before we head home."

"Oh. Yes. Good idea." She turned. "Come, Amy."

"We should get together so I can meet your husband. We don't live far from each other."

"Yeah," Mildred said. She knew how much Michael would despise Henry for not holding a real job, and for looking like that. "Well, see you then. Bye."

***

When Gretha got home at five, Freddie was painting on a small canvas next to Henry. She dropped her bag.

"Henry, you're naked!"

He looked up. "Hey. How was work?"

"Henry, is this really necessary?"

"I'm working on a new concept of creating in the nude. It brings out your vulnerability."

"Can't you do it in the morning, when our son is in school?"

"There's no shame in nudity, Gretha."

"I'm trying to teach Freddie acceptable social behavior."

He dipped the brush into the paint on his palette. "And I'm trying to unlearn him that."

"God." She rolled her eyes and walked over to ruffle Freddy's hair. "Hi there, Freddie."

He smiled up at her. "Hi Mommy. I'm hungry."

"Already? But it's not dinner time yet."

"But Daddy didn't give me lunch."

57

"Henry?"

"Mmm?" He was painting again.

"Freddie said you didn't fix lunch."

He bit the brush between his teeth and stepped back to look at the canvas. "I couldn't stop this." He motioned to the painting. "It would have broken the flow."

"He's hungry."

"It's good to sometimes feel hungry. You appreciate eating more. Besides, there are grapes. He could have eaten some if he was really starving."

Gretha took Freddie's hand. "Come, Freddie. Let's get you some dinner."

"By the way," Henry said, "Tricea called. She called a meeting with the moms. Can't remember when, though."

"Why didn't she call on my mobile?"

"She said she wanted to hear my voice. And she told me about Max."

"What about Max?"

"That we should keep Freddie away from him."

"I think I'm going to call Max's mom right now and invite him for a play date."

"I think it's very entertaining, this whole war."

"You would." Gretha left the studio, taking Freddie with her to the kitchen.

***

There were six cars parked outside the house. Cordette felt her irritation rise. Some idiot had blocked their gate. She parked her car two blocks from the house in the first available spot, and made a point of taking long, angry strides back to the house. Long before she got there, she smelled the barbeque fire and heard the music. Over the singing of an Afrikaans band, she heard male voices. She unlocked the door and banged it behind her, but there was no one to appreciate her show of annoyance.

She didn't stop to remove her coat. Walking through the lounge round the back, she saw Pieter and his friends crowed around a portable barbeque in their small backyard.

"Pieter." He didn't react. "Pieter!" He looked around, surprised. "Can I see you inside?"

Pieter crossed the lawn like a dog with his tail between his legs. The "ooooh's" and "aaaaah's" of his friends only served as fuel on her fire.

When he stood in front of her, she propped her hands on her hips. "What's going on here?"

He shrugged. "I'm just having a little *braai* with the guys."

"Without asking how I would feel about entertaining your friends? It's a week day."

"It was Jan's idea."

"So, if Jan tells you to jump into the fire, you'll do it?"

"Stop treating me like a child."

"Why don't you just get a job? Ever since you've been laid off, you've used it as an excuse to lie around, doing nothing! I'm sick of this, do you hear me?"

"That's just sweet. Why don't you try to make me feel even less of the man I already do? It's not my fault there's no work out there."

"You haven't been looking. I come home to … to this…" she waved her arms, "and when you go to bed I get to clean up the mess."

"Keep your panties on, all right? I'll clean it up." He turned and walked out the door.

"Don't you walk out on me!"

Cordette stood for another two seconds, but when Pieter resumed his place in front of the fire, a fresh beer in his hand, she felt the blood rush to her head. Her ears rang from the force.

"Bennie!"

No answer. She found him in the bathroom, smearing her make-up on the mirror, red lipstick smudges already lining the floor.

Too exhausted from anger and helplessness, Cordette

59

didn't say or do anything. Bennie looked up guiltily. Her chest started to heave. When dry sobs left her throat, Bennie escaped to the safety of his room. She looked at her reflection in the spoiled mirror. She was still wearing her thick winter coat. Her face was distorted. Slowly, she walked from room to room, observing the unmade beds and the explosion of toys and dirty clothes across the floors and furniture.

Finally, she walked through the front door and down the two blocks, got into her car and drove around. She couldn't think of anywhere to go. After thirty minutes she made a decision, returned home, let herself in and locked all the doors. She prepared a cup of noodles and fed it straight from the plastic container to Bennie. She put him to bed without a bath or brushing his teeth. She went back to their room and got undressed. She waited in the dark until she heard Pieter and his friends knocking and shouting. They would have to climb over the roof to get to the front garden. There was no other way around. She smiled, turned on her side and pretended to sleep.

***

Tricea stood on the patio, looking at the gazebo being erected in their backyard.

"There you are." Albert stepped outside, carrying two glasses of Sauvignon Blanc. He handed one to Tricea. "Everything going according to plan?"

"Of course everyone is behind schedule." She rolled her eyes. "Like always."

"It's going to be a wonderful party."

Every time the hammer that nailed the pegs into their green lawn made a noise, Albert flinched.

"It has to be," Tricea said, "for our little Johnny. Can you believe he's turning five?"

"Mmm."

"That's why everyone picks on him. He is the youngest in his class. Maybe I should have kept him back a year."

Albert sat down on the garden sofa. "No, Tricea. He was ready to go to school."

"I'm so upset that I invited Cordette's Bennie, after what Deloris told me this morning. If the invite hadn't gone out last week, I wouldn't have invited them at all."

"Cordette locked Pieter out, that's all. It's between adults. Surely you can't hold it against the child, what's his name again?"

"But children are like their parents. I don't want that kind of influence around our Johnny. And Gretha's little terror…"

Albert sighed. "What did he do, now?"

"Not him. His father. I told you."

Albert frowned.

"When I called the other day, and Henry answered…" When Albert still frowned, Tricea rolled her eyes again. "He told me he couldn't talk because he was painting naked."

Albert grinned. "Oh, that."

Tricea shot him a look. "It's not funny. He was leading me on, or something. He was obviously flirting with me. I was so insulted. And you know he swings both ways. I don't want men like that around Johnny. Can you imagi…?"

"The way you carry on, no one is good enough for Johnny."

"It's not that, Albert, but you have to be careful who your child hangs out with. They're so susceptible at this age."

"Mmm." Albert picked up the newspaper and unfolded it.

"So the other moms agree about Max. He *is* a bully. I'm going to have to see the teacher about him. I hope Cinthea finds out that there was a party and he wasn't invited. Maybe her eyes will open."

"Don't you think it sets a bad example to exclude one

child, if you have invited the whole class?"

"It's not about inviting the whole class. I invited Johnny's friends. I didn't invite Amy either."

"Is that the new girl? Why not? I thought you were taking her mother under your wing."

"There's something seriously wrong with that woman. The other morning I invited her for coffee and she stormed off. I've never been so insulted in my life. I don't want to hang around Mildred or depressed people. They only drag you down."

"So the girl is depressed?"

"No! Mildred is the mother." She gasped. "Oh, for heaven's sake! Put down that newspaper and go see what those men are doing over there. They're putting the chairs in the wrong place. And the bar was supposed to go on the east side, otherwise it'll get too much sun in the afternoon."

Albert sighed. "I'll go see."

Tricea touched her brow. "The stress of this party is going to kill me before tomorrow."

"It'll be just perfect. You always do such a great job as a hostess."

"Really?"

"Of course. My darling hostess."

He kissed her and she wrapped her arms around his neck, spilling a drop of wine down his back.

**

The other moms stood under the tree outside the school gate. Mildred's breath made vapor in the cold morning air as she rushed to meet them.

"Hi Gretha. Cordette. Deloris. What a pretty morning with the fresh snow on the mountains." She looked around. "Where's Tricea?"

"She's probably still sleeping off yesterday's party," Deloris said. "The driver dropped Johnny off this morning."

"What party?"

"Johnny's birthday party," Gretha said. "I still can't believe they made such a fuss. And that for a fifth birthday. Shocking. Now we'll be too embarrassed to invite Johnny to any of our kids' parties. There's no way we can ever live up to that."

"What was the big fuss?" Mildred said softly.

"They paid a school of actors to entertain the kids," Deloris said excitedly, "and there was a hot dog wagon for the kids. Even made candy floss and popcorn and slush puppies."

"And they had clowns on stilts and two jumping castles on the lawn," Cordette said.

Gretha snorted. "I thought the valet to park our cars was totally over the top."

"Did you see the bodyguards?" Deloris chipped in. "I don't want to know how much it must have cost. With all that money they spent they could have run the soup kitchen for two months. How many people were there?"

"All of Johnny's class," Cordette said, "minus Max of course, so that would have made twenty-seven kids and double that amount of adults, if you count all the parents."

"Yes," Gretha said, "but that still doesn't take all their family into account, and the uncles and aunts and grandparents, and there were some of Johnny's friends from the kindergarten."

"I can't believe Tricea invited his teacher," Cordette said. "That's so unheard of. It's not fair. Now she'll be biased where Johnny is concerned."

Deloris turned to a quiet Mildred. "Where were you guys?"

"We didn't know about the party," Mildred said.

The other women looked at each other.

"Oh," Cordette said, "I thought you couldn't come because Amy was sick or something."

"Tricea probably just forgot," Gretha said. "You didn't miss anything. Really."

"Sure." Mildred dipped her hands into her coat pockets. "We were busy, anyway."

"Well, now it's official," Cordette said. "Max wasn't invited, and you bet no one else will invite him to another party for the rest of the year. Everyone was talking about him being such a bully."

"I'll invite him," Gretha said.

Deloris lifted her brow. "You will?"

Gretha shrugged. "He didn't do anything to Freddie." She checked her watch. "I have to go. If I'm late for work one more day I'll get fired." She waved, rushing off.

"Well, now I can't invite Max or Freddie to Bennie's party next month," Cordette said.

"Why's that?" Deloris asked.

"Pieter thinks Henry is gay. Don't you remember that scene last year, when Gretha came home early one day and caught him with someone? And I heard it was with a man. Said it was only a model, for his art."

Deloris turned a little pale. "Wow, Cordette, since when have you become so judgmental?"

"I didn't say anything about Richard."

"I wouldn't be so fast to speak if I was the one who had the police knock down my door at one in the morning. I heard you locked Pieter and his friends out. Jan said he had to call the police on his mobile to come and threaten you to unlock the door."

"News travels fast. Who told you?"

"Jan told Richard," Deloris said.

"Well, for your information," Cordette said, "Richard's good buddy, Jan, is a bad influence on Pieter. He can't wreak havoc in his own house, so he comes to ours to do so."

"I'm not judging. I'm just saying…"

"I can't believe Amy wasn't invited," Mildred said. "Why do you think did Tricea not invite her? Was it because I didn't go for coffee with her the other morning?"

Cordette looked at Deloris. A silent look passed between them.

"I've got to go," Cordette said. She walked off without offering a greeting.

"Well, I just won't invite Johnny to Amy's party," Mildred said. "Do you want to go for a coffee, Deloris?"

"I have so much to do today. Sorry."

"When is Tommie's birthday? Amy's is in two months. You must give me tips. Looks like birthdays here are big events. So, when is Tommie's?"

"August."

"Oh, wonderful," Mildred said with forced enthusiasm. "So, Amy can look forward to her first party here soon."

"We'll see. We haven't decided what to do yet."

"Will you invite Freddie and Bennie? And Johnny?"

"I'll have to invite Johnny, won't I? Since we went to his party."

"You'll invite Amy, won't you?"

"I don't know, Mildred. I mean ... not about inviting her ... but about having the party. I don't think it's such a good idea for our Tommie to play with Bennie and Freddie too much, with what's happening. And Max ... well, I can't exactly invite him, now, least..." She shrugged. "Maybe it's better to not have a party at all."

"Maybe," Mildred said.

"Listen, I have to go. Bye, Mildred. See you around."

"I'll see you this afternoon, when we pick up the kids, won't I?"

"Maybe."

Mildred stood under the tree, suddenly alone. She stayed there for another few seconds, and then headed back to her own car. She was already late. Today, she would have to let the cleaning go, if she was to cook a decent lunch. She sat in her car for a long time and then she drove home. There was nowhere else to go, after all.

Sasq-what?
Penny Estelle

She was coming. He darted behind some bushes, hoping he hadn't been seen. That would ruin his fun and he couldn't have that. The corner of his mouth lifted into the slightest smirk. Would she scream? He hoped so.

Billowy clouds, some hanging low enough to kiss the tops of the tallest pines, hid the sun. Wind whistling through the trees and far off, low rumbling thunder would drown out any sound she would make. He held his breath as she came closer. Only a few steps more.

Her scream split the air like a knife when his hand shot out and grabbed her ankle. She fell back on her rear, scrambling backwards frantically trying to escape.

His hysterical laughter turned his sister's fear to instant rage. "You should have seen your face!" the boy gasped between peals of laughter. Andy was a twelve-year-old pain in his sister's butt.

"You're dead!" Kelly growled, pushing her long auburn hair out of her eyes. She was three years older than Andy was, but he towered over her 5-foot, 3 inch frame. Hazel eyes shot promises of pain into laughing brown ones. Kelly jumped at Andy and he zigged the other way. She stayed after him, hands reaching for anything she could grab, but coming up empty. Andy's laughter slowed him down a bit. He made an exaggerated look of fright and screamed, pretending to be her.

His Yankees baseball cap sat crooked on his head and a small leafy branch stuck in his shaggy, dark brown hair. She giggled and then burst into laughter herself. She jumped on top of him, tackling him to the ground. "Can you be any more of a nerd?" she asked.

Then they both heard it. Slowly, getting to their feet Andy whispered, "What was that?"

Kelly shook her head, goose bumps covering her body, "Let's get back to camp." They ran, looking back over their shoulders. The trees seemed to have doubled in number, closing in on them. "I think we're going the wrong way. I don't recognize anything around here!" Kelly told her brother in a panicked whisper.

Andy looked at his sister, hearing the alarm in her voice. *Drama Queen.* "Geeze, Kelly, calm yourself. I'm sure the campground is right through those trees somewhere." Andy used his thumb to point back over his shoulder because his eyes were searching the area they had just come from...listening.

"Look around, moron. We aren't even on any kind of a trail!" She whirled around, her arms wide for emphasis. "We are lost in this God-forsaken place and there's something behind us that... that..."

"Yea, what the heck was that?" Andy interrupted. "You know that scream wasn't human, don't you? His brown eyes were alive with excitement. "You know what I think it was?"

"No and I don't want to know either! Let's go," Kelly said grabbing his arm, trying to pull him along. "I didn't even want to come on this stupid camping trip but, *no*, this would be a great family bonding time," she said, using her fingers on both hands like quotations emphasizing the word bonding. "Now we are lost and who knows what is following us!"

Kelly started walking again, nodding her head. "I can see the headlines now. Pretty young girl, who had her whole life in front of her, ends up missing, never to be found again."

"What would they say about me?" Andy asked, laughing.

"You wouldn't be worth mentioning. Now come on. We need to find mom and dad."

Their search for the campground continued in silence. Kelly stopped suddenly, startling Andy from his own thoughts. "We are lost," she cried, her eyes tearing up. "We've been walking forever and all these trees look exactly the same. We could be walking in circles!"

"We aren't lost. We'll find our camp," Andy argued, none too concerned about their current predicament. He sniffed the air and scrunched up his nose. "Man, something stinks! Can you smell that?" There was definitely something and it smelled horrible! "Look up there," Andy pointed up in one of the trees. "What's that?"

They went closer to get a better look. A raccoon had been practically ripped in two. It was as though it was put there for safekeeping.

"I'm going to be sick," Kelly whimpered. "What would have done that?" She folded her arms in front of her, turning this way then that way. "It's getting late and we need to get back." She started screaming, "Mom! Dad!"

"Kelly," Andy yelled into her face, "Stop screaming! If something's out there, it will hear you!"

As if on cue, the high-pitch scream echoed through the forest. Because of the surrounding trees, the wail could have come from any direction, but it was definitely closer.

Kelly clutched Andy's arm. "What are we going to do?" she whispered.

"Run," he said. The excitement was gone, replaced by a healthy dose of fear. Andy, easily the faster runner, slowed his pace to stay close to his sister. The forest offered many obstacles; from fallen, dead trees and branches to overgrown roots and brush so thick it was almost impossible to get by.

Andy came to an abrupt stop and Kelly plowed into the back of him. "Look," he said, pointing in front of them," there's a cabin or something."

Kelly saw what her brother was pointing at and took off running, with Andy close behind. When they got there, they saw it wasn't a cabin at all, but a really old, rickety shack. The bug-eaten wood had holes big enough that they were able, to peek inside. A single hinge held on the front door and rotten shutters were the only thing that kept animals from climbing in the windows.

A loud clap of thunder boomed overhead. Both Andy and Kelly jumped and ran to push their way through the front door. Once inside, they propped the door closed, hoping the single hinge and an old metal chair would hold the door closed against the wind. Kelly stared, not moving. Andy, on the other hand, was exploring every inch of the place.

"Look!" he called. "Here's an old candle. See if you can find some matches. Check that old cupboard." Andy pointed to an old cabinet in the corner, covered with spider webs.

"No way," she told him.

With a disgusted grunt, Andy went over to look for himself. "Hey, here are some matches and some cans of beans and peaches." Andy held up dust-covered cans.

The storm was getting louder. Andy and Kelly could feel the wind blowing through some of the boards of the old shack. It wasn't cold but Kelly teeth were chattering.

Thunder cracked and then rain pounded the roof. "It's raining," Andy announced.

"Of course it's raining," Kelly said, going to stand by the lighted candle. "It always storms before the murders begin."

Laughing Andy found a rusty old can opener and gave his sister a can of peaches. Using their fingers, they ate in silence. "I'll bet mom and dad are freaking out," Kelly said.

"Yea, but they'll be so glad to see us tomorrow; they will forget to be mad!" Andy said.

"Yea, right," Kelly responded dryly.

They finished their dinner and threw the cans in the corner. "I think that scream was a Sasquatch," Andy burst out.

"Sasq-what?"

"Sasquatch, you know, Bigfoot. I read where they

have been seen in the Pacific Northwest. They are like half human half hairy monster type things.

"Andy, be quiet! I mean it! I don't need to hear this now." Kelly yelled, her voice trembling.

They were sitting against the wall when a flash of lightening lit up the shack. Kelly screamed and pointed toward the back wall. "There was something outside. I saw it."

"What was it?" Andy gasped. He tried to get up but she held him tight.

"I don't know. It looked, it looked...huge. I swear there was something there." Kelly whispered, shivering.

At that moment, the front door burst open, a light blinding both kids. "Kelly! Andy!" It was Mom.

"Mom! Dad!" The two kids were across the room and in their parents' arms. Both were talking at once. Kelly was blaming Andy and Andy was telling them about the Sasquatch.

That caught dad's attention, "The what?"

He told his parents about the scream, the dead thing up in the tree, and what Kelly thought she had seen just before they came in.

"It was probably some owl's dinner and he put it there for safekeeping," Dad said.

"No way, Dad," Andy argued. "It was gross, like something had ripped it in two and what about that really horrible scream we heard?"

"That's enough Andy. You're scaring Kelly, plus I'm not too crazy about this whole conversation, either!" his mother said.

Andy's dad agreed. "Look, it's raining pretty hard outside. Why don't we sleep here tonight and get an early start tomorrow." Everybody agreed with that idea and with mom and dad close by, Andy and Kelly went right to sleep.

The next morning the whole family woke up to the sun shining through the gaps.

The sky was blue and there was a light breeze.

Right outside the door, Kelly and Andy stopped and stared at the muddy ground. There were tracks. Foot long tracks with claws that dug deep into the mud. They started under one of the windows and trailed into the forest.

All four of them were out of breath by the time they reached the campground. The tent was down and the truck was loaded within the hour.

"Do you think they were Sasquatch tracks?" Andy asked

"No!" Mom, Dad, and Kelly replied, overly loud.

"Me, too," Andy said, looking at the forest as they drove out of the campground.

Visitor
E. B. Sullivan

Chapter One

As I drove north, my mind rambled.

After forty years of teaching, I had recently retired. To my dismay, in this elective unemployed state, a feeling of uselessness swelled, crowding out fun. My calendar bulged with events. Each day overflowed with activities both personal and civic. Yet a void existed. An intrinsic satisfaction seemed to elude me. Despite my involvements, I felt I no longer had anything of value to give to anyone.

At the height of my melancholia, my nephew Joe called to ask advice about parenting. During our conversation he commented, "Aunt Betty, you're a great role model. I admire your ability to adapt to and enjoy the many changes life presents."

His compliment nudged me into reality. Just like other transitional times, this stage would present an array of challenges as well as a multiple of rewards. I wondered how I allowed my ego to interfere with earned leisure.

Returning my focus on Joe, I asked, "Are you and your fiancée Nancy ready for your wedding?"

"I think so. Our last arrangement involves you. After me raving about your qualifications, Nancy decided she would like you to take care of her daughter Jennifer while we go on our honeymoon. I totally agree."

No longer feeling adrift, I accepted, with humble appreciation, their offer to care for Jenny.

In the subsequent weeks, it impressed me to observe how the lovestruck couple prepared Jennifer for my extended visit. Upon our first meeting, the four-year old and I instantly established a warm rapport. Still, her mother Nancy insisted I spend a weekend at their townhouse in the city. During those two days, Jenny and I took abundant pleasure in the pursuit of getting to know each other.

Since then, our phone conversations reflected her eagerness about our upcoming adventure.

During each call, Jenny asked, "Aunt Betty, will I see you today?"

"No," I replied, "but we'll be together soon."

Following the marriage ceremony, Jennifer and I would stay at Tony's log cabin located in idyllic country seclusion.

Almost there, I exited the freeway. I followed a narrow road surrounded by massive trees. Giant redwoods lined the meandering asphalt, creating a shaded tunnel. As in past visits, I marveled at the ancient vegetation.

Missing my small maneuverable car, I slowly and carefully took each curve of the winding road very seriously. Relying on her motherly instincts, Nancy recommended I rent an all-terrain SUV in case of unexpected adverse weather conditions. She feared a rainstorm could severely impede our only way out. Nancy didn't trust the hard-packed decomposed granite covering the long twisting road from the public street down through the vast acreage of the property.

I adhered to her suggestion, thinking no precaution seemed too great in protecting Jennifer.

I inched up a hill enjoying the remnants of a sunny day. On the next turn, I caught a glimpse of the picturesque retreat. Approaching the house, I slowed and parked. Before I could leave the car, Nancy stood beside me.

From the open window, I attempted to hug her. "Hi. Where's Jennifer?"

In her typical fashion, Nancy rattled off an elaborate response. "She's in her playhouse. When we're here she gets up early every morning and slips down into the root cellar where she entertains herself until I call her to breakfast."

"Joe says she would stay there night and day if we'd let her." Nancy sighed. "What's really nice is she's safe and content down there."

Half listening to her, I automatically nodded in

agreement.

With ease, I retrieved my lightweight suitcase and followed her into the house.

Nancy wanted me to hear more. "At first it really wasn't the kind of place for a little girl to spend time in, but things have come a long way since we arrived. Joe covered the unfinished surfaces with drywall, and painted the room with a lavender hue. Then I decorated the space."

As she spoke, Nancy ambled into the kitchen. "Come see it. Undoubtedly Jenny will con you into going down there with her so I'm sure you'll appreciate its present appearance."

From behind her I said, "Most of all, I just want to be with Jennifer."

Pivoting gracefully, Nancy turned toward me. A pleased grin dominated her attractive face. With one hand, she reached down as if to touch the wooden floor. From its seamless concealment in the parquet design, she raised a trap door.

In single file, we descended a short flight of creaky steps transporting us into a child's fantasy world of texture and imagination. Supple fabrics, muted colors, and a host of miniature objects beckoned me to enter this space of wonder and whimsy.

Engrossed in serious activity, Jennifer didn't seem to notice our arrival. Dressed in embroidered jeans and a lacy blouse, as if part of a painting, she fit perfectly into this artistic scene.

"Aunt Betty's here."

Looking up at us, the adorable child said, "Wow." Then like a bouncing ball, she sprung into my open arms.

After a momentary embrace, she took me over to her dolls. Beaming with pride, she introduced me to her little family.

As Nancy marched up the steps, she joked. "I can take a hint. I know when I'm not wanted."

Playful moments melted away in Jenny's happy land of make-believe.

Sometime later, her mother's cheerful voice interrupted our game by offering us an invitation. "The afternoon sun is starting to go down. Let's run outside and see if we can catch it."

I followed Jenny up the stairs, out the front door, and onto the porch. We joined her mother, who was sitting on a swing. Using wooden scraps from the cabin Joe had fashioned the oversized moving seat. Nancy added the comfortable corduroy covered cushions and contrasting pillows.

With Jenny nestled between us, Nancy and I pushed down with soles of our shoes to rock it gently.

The three of us sat in awe as we soaked up the unfolding color show of reds, purples, and crimsons.

A beguiling hush descended upon us. In delicate increments evening fell. With it, a slight chill engulfed us.

Hand in hand, we entered the dark house just as a wash of white light flashed. Its brightness illuminated the entire interior of the cozy kitchen.

"Joe's home," Jennifer piped up.

"Jenny's right. Joe will be here soon. Since this area is so off the beaten path we can actually see the beam from his headlights a few miles away."

"How intriguing," I said.

"Not really," Nancy commented in matter-of-fact tone. "You see, the start of his property is on a hill a bit higher than the one the house is on. Even though thousands of acres separate the two peaks, light can easily be seen from both points."

Following her detailed explanation, I tried to express the value of this phenomenon. "Since there's no phone service up here it must feel comforting for Joe to be able to signal you in this way."

"I guess so, but if we don't light up the cabin soon

we'll give him a real scare."

After striking one match, she skillfully lit two propane lanterns.

Chapter Two

At dawn, I awakened with expectancy. As the hours passed, caterers, relatives, and friends invaded the little house. By noon, in order to keep Jennifer clear of the commotion, I took her along with two dolls for a stroll by the stream.

"Aunt Betty I think my babies are tired."

"Then let's rest."

While we rocked her dolls to sleep Jenny asked, "Is my daddy coming to the party?"

"Honey, I don't know."

A somber expression accompanied her grown-up sounding words. "He promised to visit, but hasn't. Maybe he doesn't know where we're staying."

Not wanting her to feel rejected, I agreed. "You're probably right." As soon as the words had left my mouth, I thought it imprudent of me to give her false hope especially since I didn't know anything about this man.

"Aunt Betty, could you call him and tell him where I am?"

Instead of answering her question, I decided to elicit additional information. "What does your mother think about your father visiting?"

"Mommy doesn't like him. She says Joe is going to be my new daddy. So I don't need my old daddy anymore."

Instead of waiting for me to comment, she pointed in the direction of a nearby fir. Her face brightened. "Look at the gray squirrel. I like his big tail."

Relieved about her changing both the subject and her mood I said, "Yes, I see him. He's really cute."

Leaving her dolls behind, Jennifer ran toward the tree. "Could we take him home with us?"

Still cradling the two pretend babies in my arms, I joined Jenny. "He wouldn't be happy in a house. Squirrels like living outdoors. But speaking of homes, I guess we'd better get back to yours in order to prepare for your mother's party."

"Is it time for me to wear my new pink dress?"

"Yes indeed. Would you like to say good-bye to Mr. Squirrel before we go?"

Waving her petite hand Jennifer shouted, "Mr. Squirrel, bye, bye. I hope you stay in our trees so you can meet my daddy when he comes. I know he'll like you just as much as I do."

Chapter Three

Throughout the marriage ceremony, I stood close to Jennifer. She seemed enthralled by the lovely event.

"Mommy looks just like one of my Barbie dolls. Doesn't she?" Jennifer asked.

"I think your mom looks even prettier." I gave her a little squeeze. "And so do you Jenny."

She leaned her little body into me and said, "I like weddings. Maybe Mommy can get married again next week."

Her innocent remark initially made me laugh, but then a tinge of sorrow clouded my joyful disposition.

These two young adults had previously suffered through the pangs of separation and divorce. I could only hope Nancy and Joe had gleaned enough wisdom from their past struggles to make this new union a lasting one.

With the sacred rites complete, the party began. Despite the absence of electricity and many other modern day conveniences, the reception proved to be a huge success. Musicians performed toe-tapping tunes, delectable delicacies were prepared over an open fire pit, and the great outdoors provided an amazing ambiance.

At dusk, the last of the guests and crew departed.

Within the cabin, subdued murmurings of love slipped through the rounded walls as the bride and groom changed their clothes.

I helped Jennifer with her shower. As she put on her pajamas, she asked if she could sleep in her playhouse. After chatting for a while, Jenny easily agreed it would be better for her to rest in her own room.

When the newlyweds entered her space, I gazed at the enchanting pair. Dressed in matching outfits of blue jeans and white tee shirts they personified true bliss.

Together these attentive parents read their child her favorite story. By the time the couple decided to depart,

Jennifer was already tuckered out. From underneath her pastel coverlet she dreamily whispered goodnight to her mother and new stepdad.

As the couple left the house, I walked a few steps behind them and overheard Nancy say, "I feel uneasy about leaving."

Joe tried to reassure her. "Don't worry. Out here in the woods, Jenny's far from harm's way."

Before I could confirm his sentiments, they were in their four-wheel drive SUV.

From the raised porch, I watched the rearview lights of their vehicle fade into the pitch of night. The sound of their engine droned on long after all visible traces of them vanished. I waited to catch a glimpse of the red beams to reappear when the car reached the highest hill, but for some reason I never saw any sign of them. After waiting and watching for several more minutes, I guessed the taillights were not bright enough to project across the distance. Not questioning my conjecture any further, I slipped into the house.

Later on, I sat outside enjoying the country stillness. Sipping some hot tea, I reflected upon the beautiful day. Among the many strangers, Jennifer exhibited her friendly nature. I realized she could have comfortably stayed with a host of other people. A hushed gratitude caused my eyes to moisten. By choosing me to watch her precious daughter, Nancy created an endearing bond between us.

My gaze turned to the pages of a novel. Under the limited amount of light emitted from a propane lantern, my tired eyes quickly faltered and dissuaded me from reading. At ten o'clock, I extinguished all the lights, entered my room, and ensconced with contentment, crawled under toasty warm blankets.

Chapter Four

A flash of light caused me to bolt straight up in bed. The dial of a battery-powered clock illuminated a scarlet 2:00 a.m.

Remembering Nancy's earlier account, I knew a vehicle headed for the house. Although it didn't seem logical for the couple to disturb us in the middle of the night, I attempted to calm myself by thinking they needed to fetch an important item before traveling.

Persistent waves of protectiveness washed over me. A recurrent question resounded in my head. *What if someone else approached?*

Almost without thinking, I slipped into my robe, rushed into the kitchen, and opened the door to the root cellar. In bare feet, I ran into Jennifer's room. I whisked the child up into my arms and carried her down the squeaky steps. She moaned slightly as she smiled through her deep sleep. For a few brief moments, I held her close. I rocked her until her breathing was steady and deep. Gently I laid her slender form on the tiny chenille covered settee.

Drenched in cold sweat, I returned to the kitchen and closed the hatch door. From an adjacent room I grabbed an area rug to cover the latch. An instant later, it occurred to me instead of hiding the security spot, I was drawing attention to it.

For a second time I snatched up the rug. As if pitching a ball, I flung it high in the air. It landed on the sofa with a soft thud.

Sitting still in the darkness, I waited. All the while, I attended to the outside noises.

Had they been there all along?

Besides the chatter from a multitude of crickets, the wind rustled the treetops and the stream played a refreshing song. At another time, this collective tranquil hum would have soothed me. Right then, these combined natural melodies initiated an annoying agitation. I feared they would conceal sounds from an intruder.

How wrong I was.

The thunderous roar of an engine jolted my store of adrenalin.

This rude disturbance caused me to reformulate my plans.

Remembering Joe once told me he stored a shotgun in the attic, I stumbled around until I found the dangling rope attached to the captain's stairs. Strength found its way into my arms. I pulled down the heavy steps, hoisted myself up the narrow portal, and retrieved the loaded weapon along with a box of shells. I tucked the box in my pocket. Its weight dragged down the left side of my robe. As I moved, it bounced off my thigh as if to remind me of both its presence and its dangerous potential.

Although contrary to my pacifist philosophy, I felt convinced this represented the wisest choice. It occurred to me when put to the test my beliefs were easily swayed. I settled my moral dilemma by rationalizing. Certainly saving the child was a valid excuse to seize any available means of self-defense.

Without further hesitation, I lowered myself into the fanciful retreat and drew the trap door above my head to a close. In the cool darkness, I clutched the wooden stock. My tense body matched its rigid structure.

Chapter Five

I remained huddled on the hidden staircase. During what seemed like an inordinate period the mechanical noise grew to a deafening pitch until the ground underneath me shook. Minutes clicked by.

An abrupt silence, like a roar of thunder, awakened an ominous sensation to vibrate within me. I sucked in my breath.

A squeaking began, ending with a slam. My mouth opened. To prevent it from emitting a scream, I forced air to escape from my expanded lungs.

Several intervals of knocking were accompanied by a masculine, voice. "I know it must be late, but I've traveled so far. You must let me in."

Competing with his rapid taps on the window, he bellowed. "Look, I'm not here to scare or hurt anyone! You have to believe me! Just give me what I want. Then I'll leave you alone."

With his emphatic message, the faint pounding grew louder and the floorboards above my head growled.

With blood-curdling certainty, I knew this horrid man entered the cabin. I aimed the weapon toward the closed trap above me. My right index finger laced itself around the cold metal trigger.

His reverberating rough voice yelled, "This doesn't have to take long."

As he moved from room to room, his voice drifted. I strained my ears to hear him.

"Where are you? This place isn't very big. Don't you realize sooner or later I'll find you?"

Listening to crashing and clanking noises above I conjured up visions of him ransacking, and vandalizing this appealing home.

Meanwhile, here I was. Not knowing for how long, anxious and trembling, I sat in the dimness.

His voice and footsteps stopped. I heard the door close with a bang.

With great concern, I checked on Jennifer. I realized that like other children this dear one could sleep through just about anything.

Hearing her rhythmic breathing calmed me down long enough to think on a more rational basis.

Moments dragged by in silence. This man probably would not leave until he obtained whatever he came here to get. Not to place Jennifer at risk, I needed to seize the opportunity to confront him while she slept. Once she awakened, he would discover her. What would happen then?

My gut told me I needed to act immediately. Once I discovered what he wanted, I could give it to him. His words had told me he would leave.

Could it be that simple? Could I believe him?

Chapter Six

Praying I had assessed the situation correctly, I slowly raised the trap door. In stealthy movements, I crawled out onto the kitchen floor. My fingers closed the hatch in slow increments. Gradually I slithered across the smooth wooden surface toward the uncovered window.

Rising my head to eye level, I peered into the blackness. I blinked a few times, but as if I were blind, I couldn't see a thing. From above came a beam of light. Looking toward the sky the full moon peeked out from underneath a passing cloud. In direct line of sight, I spied a dark nondescript pickup truck.

I turned and caught a glimpse of a figure sitting on the swing. A churning whirlpool of terror, like an acid, burned my skin. Even in his hunched position, he appeared enormous. Much larger than any person I had ever seen. His head buried in his two oversized hands obscured his face.

As I stared at him, I began to feel his vulnerability. Without considering another thought, I rose. With one long stride, I reached the door, grabbed its brass handle, and opened it.

The man brazenly stepped out onto the porch.

Pointing the menacing shotgun at the intruder, I managed to spit out, "Don't you even think about moving."

Just as he raised his head, the light disappeared. Once again, clouds blocked the moonlight. What I saw amounted to a vague outline of a man.

"Who are you?" he asked hoarsely

My stomach quivered. "The question is, who are you?"

"Nobody," he retorted.

"Well, whoever you are, take small steps and walk to your truck. Get going or I'll pull the trigger."

His feet went backward until he sat on the swing.

"Didn't you hear me? Get out of here before I kill you."

Sincere conviction accompanied his words. "Please do me that favor. Go ahead. Just blow me away."

Ignoring his request, I demanded, "What do want?"

His despondent voice whispered, "It doesn't really matter. Does it?"

"Let me be the judge of that." The heavy weapon bobbed up and down within my nervous grip.

"What I want is the one thing I can't have."

This strange giant wept. As if in a state of tortured anguish, his repetitive wailing echoed a deep sense of suffering.

Not wanting to be fooled by his melodramatic display, I interrupted his crying by repeating, "Will you please just tell me what this is all about?"

After a short time, he ended his lament replacing it with a growling inflection. "It's about my daughter Jenny. I want to see her."

In response to his hostile tone, an acute annoyance flared up within me. Indignation seemed to temper my fright. Demanding answers, I yelled at him. "If you're her father, why would you sneak up here like a thief in the night? Why wouldn't you just call Nancy and make proper arrangements to see your beautiful child?"

Like an enraged bear ready to strike, he raised his colossal form. The snarling quality of his voice matched his fierce countenance. "Why? 'Cause the judge ordered me to stay away from both Nancy and my Jenny. Sure I'm no saint, but no matter what I've done, I've never been a threat to my own child."

"So you're violating a court order in addition to scaring the wits out of me."

He quieted his voice a bit. "Not exactly. Nancy went on and on in front of His Honor's bench. Finally, to shut her up, the judge suggested I stay away for a while.

Well, I obeyed him. When our next court date arrived, Nancy's attorney arranged for a postponement.

"All these months later I still haven't seen my little girl."

He bowed his head. Through his sniffles, I heard the sounds of genuine sadness.

"Lady, I'm sorry. This was a crazy idea. Let me ease back into my truck and out of your life."

With slow short steps, I moved a few paces backward. With the long gun barrel, I motioned him forward.

Like a dejected pup, he lumbered toward his vehicle.

A grating noise came from the heavy door as he swung it open. A light from the cab revealed glistening tears streaming down his face.

"Sorry," he said.

In the unnatural glare, an ashen cast descended upon him like a ghostly shroud. Color drained from his skin and his tremendous strength seemed to wither away.

The gravity of his expression alerted me to the depths of his depression. Sympathetic to his situation, I convinced myself only I could help this desperate man.

"Wait," I cried out. "I'll let you see Jennifer for a few minutes. But one false move and you're a dead man."

His chin lifted. "What are you saying? When and where can I see her?"

"Right here. This morning when she wakes up."

His face, like a rubber mask, took on a different persona. Although streaked with fresh tears, it conveyed the essence of joy.

Nodding my elbow in the direction of the front door, I ordered, "Come inside and get cleaned up."

Chapter Seven

Like an obedient child, the strange man let himself into the small dwelling and stood before the porcelain basin.

I temporarily placed the gun on the table. Contorting my body, I attempted to lean over it. Through my robe, the box of shells banged against the table leg. I wondered if he realized what caused the thumping noise.

Since anxiety spilled out to my shaky fingers, it took several attempts before I successfully struck a match.

In the faint light, I could see him reach out. "Here let me light the lantern."

I screamed, "Don't come any closer!"

He froze in place.

Once illumination flooded the space, I salvaged the weapon.

He continued to stand absolutely still until I pointed the barrel toward the sink.

I felt more at ease when he proceeded in its direction.

With water splashing and soapsuds bubbling, he ducked his entire head under the faucet. Still dripping wet, he turned and faced me.

After a few seconds, I realized he needed a towel. I pulled one out of a cabinet drawer and handed it to him.

"Perhaps you'd like to take a nap in there." I pointed the gun at the door to my room.

In way of acknowledging my suggestion, he slipped into the guest quarters.

Left standing alone in the kitchen, I felt my blood gushing through my veins as it loudly pumped through an aching heart.

What was this all about?

Joe had never mentioned an abusive ex-husband. Jennifer referred to her father in the most positive way.

Nancy could act a bit theatrical at times, but she didn't strike me as the kind of woman who would deliberately hurt anyone, least of all Jennifer. She must have good reason to keep Jenny away from her dad.

Then why did I believe this man? Why did I let him stay? At any rate, this business didn't concern me. My role here didn't give me the right to decide who should or shouldn't see Jennifer.

Paranoid thoughts spun in my exhausted brain. I imagined Jenny's father to be a person who from time to time experienced unpredictable episodes of irrational, maniacal behavior. Then again, this man could be just about anyone only pretending to be a loving parent. He could be a common thief or someone under the influence of mind-altering narcotics.

Totally convinced I must force him to vacate the premises, I began to formulate a new strategy when a sweet voice interrupted me. "Auntie ,where are you? I need to use the bathroom."

Trying not to make noise, I gingerly placed the gun on the floor. I pulled open the concealed door, and climbed down the short flight of steps. In the shadowy light, I could see her face. A protective impulse pleaded with me to wrap her up in my arms, carry her to the car, and drive far away. Since I had tossed the keys to the SUV on the dresser in the room where the stranger slept, it seemed impossible to remove her from this potentially perilous scene.

"Jenny, sweetheart, take my hand. I'll bring you to the bathroom."

She lingered, trying to decide on a toy to carry with her.

Remembering I left the gun on the kitchen floor, I wanted to enter the room alone so I could stow it away without her knowing.

"Jenny, wait on the bottom step until I call you. Then you can go use the restroom."

In her grogginess, she mechanically obliged.

I climbed the steps and lifted the hatch. Before I could see him, I felt his clammy touch.

"Let me help you." His manly voice assaulted my ears.

"Daddy, Daddy, I knew you would come," Jennifer squealed.

In a flash, we three were in the kitchen. Jenny snuggled up in her father's embrace while I frantically searched the room for the shotgun.

All my worst fears came crashing down on me as I heard Jenny say, "Did you come to take me away with you while Mommy's gone?"

A bizarre grin flashed across his face.

That was it. This four-year old figured it out. He came here to kidnap her, and I had foolishly given him the opportunity to do so.

Chapter Eight

Standing next to me in the kitchen, still holding Jenny, the stranger chuckled. Then he reminded the child, "Don't you need to use the bathroom?" He lowered her feet to the floor.

As Jennifer ran to relieve herself, he urgently explained, "I know this looks bad, but to avoid Jenny from seeing it I stashed the gun in the bedroom closet." His eyes bulged and his lips curled up, giving him a hideous appearance, but his subsequent statement sounded authentic. "Believe me, I'm not going to hurt you."

At a loss for words, I just stared at him.

Within moments, Jenny ran back into his awaiting arms. Even in the diffused light, I could see her entire form exuding happiness. Glancing at her dad's face, I witnessed a similar glow.

It seemed clear I was invisible to both of them as they reveled in their reunion.

Like it or not, I had done what I had done.

The two of them headed for Jenny's playroom. I followed, sat down, and akin to an unseen phantom, watched father and daughter reacquaint.

They participated in a series of pretend scenarios. During a tea party similar to a male version of Alice in Wonderland, he sat on a dwarf chair next to a diminutive table.

Every so often, he peered at his child with an extraordinary intensity. Before this date, I had never observed any parent study his offspring with such scrutiny. It appeared as if he attempted to catalogue the many developmental changes, which had occurred during his long absence.

Hours passed.

Bright sunlight streamed down into the root cellar from a small high corner window. It replaced the sepia luminescence from the propane lantern. Intruding upon their laughter, I offered to prepare breakfast.

His eyes sparkled, when he said, "I'll fix us something."

Her father lifted Jennifer into his arms, and carried her up the stairs. "What would you like to eat, honey?"

Jenny just shrugged her shoulders.

He perused the pantry, pulled out a box of cereal, poured some in a bowl. Next, he skinned a banana, and made a silly face from its ripeness over the flakes. His creativity provoked a very pleasant reaction from Jennifer. With apparent pleasure, she consumed all of her food.

Their merriment resumed. Giggles and smiles dominated their interactions. Showering her with tender love, he made a positive impression. In all this gaiety, he certainly didn't appear to be a villain. I attempted to excuse his trespassing into this very house only a few hours earlier, by blaming his actions on his high level of frustration.

From the corner of my vision, I noticed Jennifer yawning. She rubbed her eyes.

Alerted to her signs of fatigue her father announced, "Because there's much work to be done I must go now."

He kissed Jennifer good-bye. While he transferred her into my arms he said, "Thanks for this great gift."

I felt a hot flush splash from my cheeks to my lips. I nodded and smiled at him.

With his shoulder, he politely held the door open for us to step outside.

For some reason it seemed important for me to ask, "Don't you even want to know who I am?"

First, he smiled at Jennifer. Then he made eye contact with me. "For some time now I've known you're a living saint."

His flattery reinforced my conviction. I felt I had made the right decision in allowing him to visit Jenny.

The little body in my embrace began to wriggle.

"Let me down," she squealed.

Understanding her desire to hug him again, I lowered Jennifer onto the weathered surface.

With small running steps, she started to follow her father.

His voice conveyed firm authority. "Jenny, you stay right there on the porch. I promise we'll be together real soon."

In haste, I reached Jennifer and placed my hands on each of her tiny arms. She didn't seem to notice either my touch or the puddles of cold dew beneath her feet.

Concurring with him, I offered, "I'll do everything in my power to help you keep your promise."

While he slowly nodded, his features projected sternness as he said, "Damn right you will."

Before I could respond, Jenny wriggled from my gentle grip. Her fingers pointed to the forest while her lips shouted, "Daddy, Daddy, look up in the big tree. It's my friend, Mr. Squirrel."

Her father did not acknowledge his sweet child.

Instead, his truck door groaned as he opened and closed it.

Perhaps it was just the reflection of the sun on his windshield, but he appeared to have a glazed look on his face.

In order to get his attention I took a few long strides past Jennifer.

By then he had backed up and was turning his truck around.

Chapter Nine

I carried Jennifer and her favorite doll to the SUV and placed her in her car seat. My sweaty fingers struggled to fasten the security buckles.

"We're going to take a short trip," I said.

"Good. I like going places."

I cautiously drove downhill over the hard-packed road.

During the entire ride, Jennifer talked nonstop. Several times, she said, "I'm so happy Daddy came to visit."

Too busy concentrating, I didn't comment or respond.

Once we twisted through the tree-lined streets, I felt a bit relieved. "We're almost in town," I told Jenny.

"Goody."

At the police station, the almost deserted lot gave me plenty of parking options.

"Jenny, you stay with the nice officer while I speak to the man in charge." I left her at the reception desk and entered Chief Larson's office.

As if in a trance, I told him about my unexpected visitor.

In conclusion, I recounted, "As Jenny's father accelerated his truck, the wind lifted a tarp covering its bed. Standing on the raised porch, a vivid image registered in my mind—Nancy and Joe, heaped together like old rag dolls, had matching daggers protruding from their bloodstained T-shirts."

Lost
Barbara Weitzner

He looks up and realizes the hand he is holding is not his grandfather's, his heart beating in a jittery manner. At the same moment, the man looks down and pulls his hand away from the boy. "Hello, young fellow, are you lost?" he asks in a concerned, friendly way.

Without answering, the boy runs away, remembering Grandpa's warning about not talking to strangers; strangers who could kidnap him, torture him, murder him. And his family will never know.

He assures himself Grandpa will never go home without him, and immediately feels better about things. Grandpa will be so happy to find me, he'll buy me peanuts and bubble gum. His eyes search the crowded aisle of the circus sideshow for the beloved, familiar face he has known all seven years of his life. He tries to call but his voice isn't very strong. He says a silent prayer to be found, and begins to work up a sweat even though the summer day is chilly. People are moving back and forth in every direction, voices floating over him for there is so much to see. Each step demands a decision, turn right or left? This way or that way? He trudges past bright and cheerful families, some stopping to view an exhibit, an old woman reading tarot cards, a half-man half-woman, a huge guy lifting weights, some lining up to take a ride on the Ferris wheel, the merry-go-round, a shooting gallery, the roller coaster, his favorite. People too busy having fun to notice him, to realize he is alone and lost. It's not fair—all those kids having fun. Don't cry, you're too old to cry, he tells himself. What now, he wonders. He is at a loss for what to do. A crowd is bunched around another booth selling souvenirs. He and Grandpa had already stopped to look at all the dumb stuff, except for the kaleidoscope he decided to buy later with the five dollars his dad gave him.

He enters what appears to be a food court. People are licking ice cream cones, sipping colas. He smells popcorn and hot dogs. He looks around, eyes seeking everywhere. A family brushes past making his grandpa's absence more acute. As soon as he finds him, he will tell him how much he loves him, stuff he's always been too shy to say. He'll thank him for the many times he made him laugh, or read him a story, or taught him checkers. If only I had a cell phone like some of the kids in my class, he thinks. But Dad said I'm too young and too careless. He knows it's true. Dad's right, I lose a lot of stuff. Like the keys to the house. Stuff like that. He decides that as soon as he gets home he will start taking better care of his things.

He leaves the food court. Picking up his pace, he walks the aisles which are filled with people, none of whom he recognizes. In no time, Grandpa is going to find me and we'll continue having fun. There's nothing to worry about, he assures himself over and over again.

Two girls about his sister's age pass him laughing, lost in some private joke. He peeks inside the first tent he comes to and blushes. He is unaccustomed to seeing ladies in their underwear. They stop chattering and glare at him. He can't stop himself from staring at all the boobs pushing out of bras, the belly buttons peeking above lacy panties. He realizes he needs to blink and does. "Beat it, kid," a women balancing on one leg, the other leg already inside her costume, snaps. He'd like to tell this to Jake, his best pal, whose crazy ideas always get them in trouble.

Outside, the crowd swerves as one, moving aside to allow an oompah band to parade by. Now he has no idea where he is. He wants to shout. He wants to stay calm. He's not a baby. He's scared. He stops to rest in the shadows of what appears to be a poster of a tattooed lady. He wonders why Grandpa hasn't found him. "I don't think Grandpa will go home without me," he says aloud. Maybe he ought to tell someone, but who?

Two kids spot him, the type Mom warned him against talking to. Beavis and Butthead.

"Hi, kid, got any money? Weed?" They stand in his

way stopping him from passing them. He shakes his head, feels his face turning red, aware of how dumb he looks in his Spider-Man T-shirt. "I don't have any money so beat it and leave me alone."

Now why did he say that? He intended to sound cool, but his voice came out squeaky. He feels a sudden surge of fear and has to fight back tears. They are bullying him and he feels defenseless. They break out laughing. Beavis leans so close to his face the boy can smell the sauerkraut on his breath and see the zits on his chin. No way he's telling them he's lost Grandpa.

"Let's see what ya got hidin' in yah pants, kid." Butthead grabs a fistful of the boy's T-shirt. The five dollars his dad gave him is folded in his pocket. The boy surprises them by darting around Butthead and runs for his life. He moves to join a crowd of people chattering in a foreign language, makes himself calm, walks among them, and finds himself looking back to check if Beavis and Butthead are following him.

A green and white striped tent stands by itself. He lifts the flap. The inside is dark. It is empty and seems to be used for storage. He's out of breath and can't think of anything better to do, not wanting to rejoin the crowds outside. He'd gotten up early, anxious to be ready when Grandpa came for him, which now seems a long time ago, when his sister had yelled at him for waking her, even though he'd tried not to make any noise. He needs to rest and catch his breath. It will be safe here, he thinks. I'll stay here for a while until I'm sure Beavis and Butthead are gone. The quiet and soft darkness help. He feels his way over to a wall, slides down the side until he's sitting on the dirt floor, wriggles his back against the side until it isn't too uncomfortable, stretches his legs, and considers the shame of being a lost kid. His sense of isolation grows. If Grandpa finds me, I promise to do better in math. How many times he's fallen asleep at his desk while Miss Kathi was writing the times tables on the blackboard?

To keep from crying he hums the tune from Frozen, a movie Grandpa took him to see that he loved. It helps him. He wishes he were home with his family, even his mean older sister who is never in a good mood. He should be used to it by now but he isn't. Maybe she has her reasons—he's never thought about it this way. Grandpa had tried to get her to come along but she preferred to go another time with her friends. She'd been wearing a shirt he remembers had been their mom's. He's seen the same helpless grief in his sister but they've been powerless to console each other. He thinks about the sadness when his mom got sick and died, the worst day of his life. He yearns to have a mother again and knows he can never ever have his wish. And though she has been gone two years, he can't stop loving her, even though she will be dead for the rest of his life. "Don't be sad," she'd whispered to him, "I will always be watching over you." As his mom worsened, Grandpa was the one who sat with him and explained what was happening. The hardest part was understanding why. And now his dad's always sad and not smiling very often and seems to prefer spending his time alone. No more tossing the football back and forth or reading comics together. It's not as if he'd chosen his sister over him, he never even noticed that she'd straightened her hair. One minute we were a whole family and the next minute not. For a while their house was full of people bringing so much food that Gram had to throw some away. He can picture mom's face, helping him to blow out the candles on his birthday cake, even after more than a year. "I'm not a baby. I won't cry," blinking furiously to stop his tears. He wipes his nose with the hem of his T-shirt.

These are the thoughts imprisoned in the tiredness of his body; he nods off.

A scraping sound awakens him, he thinks he's heard a sound. He listens, it is quiet. Then a movement.

There again, the sound, a scuffing. Mice? Rats? He is terrified of rats; knows a kid who caught one and kept it for a pet until the thing bit him and the kid had to go through some kind of painful shots. How long has he slept? It feels like he's been here for hours. He begins to feel nervous— shouldn't have fallen asleep. Should have stayed outside where Grandpa could find him. He doesn't want to be alone in here anymore. He scrambles up, dusts off his jeans, and runs out of the tent. Not as many people about now as he makes his way back to the main aisle where he'd last saw Grandpa.

"Bobby? Is that you, Bobby? I was very worried."

Grandpa apologizes to him as if it was his fault. The boy gives a shuddering tear-filled sigh. Now he is smiling. He takes the gnarled old hand and kisses it. It is time to forget.

The Tin Foil Hat Society
Cynthia Ley

Mark Carmichael knew there were real life aliens. He knew it because there *had* to be.

Unlike his parents, Mark hadn't grown up reading pulp science fiction and stories of thinly disguised misogynists who dressed in funny costumes and came from other worlds, and whose sole purpose was to tease his sexual urges.

No. Mark knew there were aliens because all the conspiracy theorists said so. He knew they were right because the conspiracy theorists, for all their covertness, were frequently more accurate than any story you might find any night on good old trustworthy NBC news. Take the Siriuns, for instance.

He knew that Puma Punku had been constructed by a master race from Sirius who were very serious about their engineering expertise.

He knew that the Nazca lines were a prank played by the same folks from Sirius, because they thought it would be funny to watch humans try to figure out the great and mystical meanings of their marginal doodlings. To this day, the Siriuns were still laughing it up.

As for the folks who said that Earth evolved on its own, thank you very much, without any help, intercession, or intervention from superior beings from outer space— they were nuts. Anyone with half a brain knew that Earth was one of many planets the Siriuns had seeded. Although, Mark conceded, culling the herd was overdue. Some folks were major wastes of DNA, through no fault of their own. Maybe the Siriuns wanted them to take care of it.

At least that was what his girlfriend Peggy Janick said.

And anyway, Mark had grown up with a Border Collie. He knew it was smarter than he was.

***

The club met every Friday night, over at Jack Scott's. Jack had started the group back in 1999, when everyone was waiting for The End to hit at twelve midnight in their time zone on New Year's eve. Nothing happened, save that the bars and churches were busier than usual. Jack called his group together, plus a few converts, and consulted the star charts, the latest readings from NASA, the current Hubble images, and tapped into the lines at SETI.

Jack swore that in the static of electromagnetic space noise he heard "NEXT CYCLE" being tapped out in Morse code, and took it to mean that The End was going to take place on the turn of the year to 2001. "It's not The End, folks," he swore. "It'll be a time of great transformation and rejoicing. We'll see our Creators face to face!"

Everyone grinned, nodded, and passed the champagne.

They spent the next year carefully tracking Sirius, having long ago accepted the idea that the constellation was the point of origin for all life on Earth. Much to their joy, they discovered that Sirius would be at its brightest the night of December 31, 2000.

It was going to be one helluva party. Jack even wrote back, after calculating the time it would take for his message to reach the stars. 'WELCOME. EAGERLY AWAITING ARRIVAL."

Meanwhile, back at SETI, a tech listening in shrugged and figured it was just another nutcase from Roswell making plans for a holiday bash.

***

New Year's Eve. The Night of Nights.

The gang congregated at Jack's place as usual, armed to the teeth with chicken wings, chips, and thermosfuls of espresso. They all looked at each other, taking a mental roll.

Jack, of course. The brains of the operation, had worked for a major observatory back in the day. The stuff he'd seen in the sky had made him a believer long ago.

His wife had wished he'd noticed that the lawn needed mowing and the car was leaking oil. She'd split years ago for someone more down to earth.

Rob, their twenty-five year old son, shared his old man's enthusiasm, even if he was a bit superstitious about it. It always worried him that the Siriuns might be offended by their surveillance. "Uh…they've got spaceships and shit," he'd say.

Jack would always laugh good-naturedly and put an arm around his shoulders. "Now why would they want to blow us up, Son? Hell, they put us here!"

Larry Sousa. Larry was a 40-something fringie, but not in the sense of being a skeptic. Larry wanted to believe everything. It made him happy. "Listen to yer dad, kid," he'd offer by way of advice.

Larry's wife Barbara was just happy to play along. The people were a little whacko, but nice enough and it kept peace in her house. Besides, there were times when it was downright interesting, if a bit odd. Odd was sexy. Described Larry to a T.

Roger and Mary Rollins. Mary had fallen in love with the universe the instant the first Hubble photos hit the public eye. To her, the sky was the limit, and it was limitless.

Roger was an engineer and loved maps and charts and math problems. He helped Jack plot out light trajectories and the time it took for light to get from one place to another. He was designing a spacecraft that could ride the time warp to Sirius because he wanted to go there.

Peggy Janick. Mark's girlfriend, college senior majoring in archaeology. She thought the seeding theory was fascinating. What was even more fascinating to her was the idea of ancient alien relics and the role aliens might have had in determining the evolution of *homo sapiens.*

Mark, Peggy's classmate, thought the idea of

sentient human beings was flat-out hilarious, ancient or not. He was more inclined to think that aliens would be interested in having a self-propagating workforce, but that Peg might be right about them having a role in getting the species beyond being nit eating butt scratchers. Now they were beer swilling butt scratchers.

At least brewing took some science.

***

They tugged on coats, scarves, caps, and gloves. Backpacks were checked for binoculars and cameras, jacket pockets for cell phones. They were ready.

"Don't forget your hats," Jack reminded everyone as they prepared to leave. He packed up his telescope and handed it to Rob, then grabbed his star charts, rolling them up efficiently and dropping them into a long cardboard tube.

"I brought a few extra rolls of heavy duty," Barb said. She was always so organized.

"Shiny side out!" Mary chirped, not to be outdone. "Don't want to get caught by those high pitched transmissions!"

Mark wondered what that would be like. So did Peggy. They looked at each other, and winked.

They made their final calculations and set off for the valley backroads where the only landbound lights they would see belonged to a coyote.

***

The winter night could not have been more perfect, more conducive to stargazing. There was no wind save the exhalations of nervous anticipation.

Hats were donned, glinting in the dark.

Sirius in all its brilliant glory.

Mark and Peggy stared at the brightest light in the heavens. They took off their hats. They looked into the galaxy of each other's eyes. They clasped hands and walked off into the deep brush.

Mating season.

They were never heard from again.

***

Later, Jack Scott would tell the police that a blinding white light had come down from the heavens and sucked them up like a black hole powered vacuum cleaner. Mary, Barb and the rest all backed him up. "But it was their fault," Mary said brokenly, looking skyward. "They removed their hats—" She broke down sobbing, and had to be escorted to a car by a cop who kindly lent her his handkerchief.

Rob swore up and down that their disappearance was "some serious shit, man," and was reminded by his dad that "some serious shit" hardly described what happened. "I dunno," he said, shaking his head.

Barb said that the last thing she saw of the college kids was when they wandered off. She didn't think anything of it at the time. It was a beautiful night to make out.

Roger had been deep in his figures when his wife nudged him and gestured towards the kids. He remembered her saying something about, "Do you want to...?" but she never finished the sentence because that was when all hell broke loose.

That, Jack said, was when every coyote for a mile around took up howling. Never heard anything like that before in his life. Then there was that crazy light, then utter silence.

They split up and went looking for Mark and Peg.

All they found were their backpacks.

And lots of pawprints.

The coyotes had vanished too.

Their heavy-duty all-purpose tin foil hats were found lying on a bush, adorning it like some absurd Christmas ornaments.

***

"So where do you think they went?" the lead cop asked.

Jack looked bemusedly at him. "Are you serious?"

Summer Rain
Silvia Villalobos

It all began when Mom made her announcement. "This summer we're taking the vacation we've been talking about, Lia," she said. "To the beach, in a tent. Camping all summer long, so bring lots of books."

Rolling my eyes, I spewed out my teenage wisdom, "I'm sixteen. I have a life."

Undeterred, Mom described our trip to Oceano, California. We wouldn't be using transportation to explore the area, she explained. In fact, we would not be leaving the campgrounds, and will depend on what we bring and the bare necessities within the facility. We would be walking, fishing with Dad. There would be storytelling, campfires. When bored, we would be reading.

"No electronics during this trip," she continued, her smile intact. "We live in a world of sensory abundance and bonding poverty. This vacation will make up for that."

The anger felt bitter on my lips. "No high school student dumps everything and goes away for the summer without a cell phone."

But that was exactly what I did. I took my summer, wrapped it into oily rags, poured gasoline on it, and lit a match.

Now, sitting in the shuttle van on our way to the stupid campsite, the California sun setting my eyeballs on fire, I leaned my head on the window and closed my eyes. Sure, I loved camping, some camping, anyway, and books, but why travel all the way to California from Seattle for the *whole* summer to read?

I hated this trip with the fire of a thousand suns fueled by the souls of vengeful demons. What about my hangout club? What about cute Joey who liked me?

When I had asked, Mom shoved yet more torture down my throat. "Take plenty of clothes but don't worry about rain gear. There is no summer rain in California." She smiled that tolerant smile of hers. "We'll be washing everything by hand, frying fish on a propane stove, cooking on a grill. It will be fun."

The van dumped us at the main gate of *Camp Oceano*. Flipping wonderful. The big wonder of beach camping, where the breeze slapped my face like a bitter witch, was upon us. Blown by the wind and baked by the sun, with no electronic devices to numb the pain, to transport me into the world of the living, back home.

Thirty minutes later, I found myself on the rocky beach along the Pacific Ocean, in a place so quiet I could hear the earth's pulse. The moaning of the sea.

Nothing but the sky and the ocean opened up before us. Sand, water, and canvas tents. All we needed was an army of bugs and flies to attack like in some horror movie. Show Mom what it's like to live with the insects.

Sitting cross-legged in a tent no larger than a closet, I spend my first two days protesting my imprisonment by reading. That's what I came here for, right? Read, nap, and eat, with bathroom breaks. There wasn't much to do after sundown, when temperatures did a fifty degree flip, but sit by the fire. I tried hiding inside the tent, letting my mind fall into oblivion, but I'd hear Mom and Dad talk to the elderly couple next to us over wine. Blabbering about times gone by and the song of dolphins.

Prisoner to nights longer than forever and cold mornings that gave way to hot days. Even the weather was all over the place, moody. Angry at the world, like me.

Now and then, the wind brought over sounds, but I refused to let them in. Screw nature and sensory whatever. I will sit here and count the hours, days and weeks, my silent misery heard loud and clear.

The third evening, high-pitched sounds broke past my resistance barrier. Laughter and undeciphrable words. People speaking in different languages. Young voices.

Reluctant, I unzipped my tent flap. Three teenagers walked past, their happiness irking yet tantalizing. One of them caught my eye, the red-haired girl. I stepped out, kicked the sand with my foot. I looked out at the setting sun leaving an orange ball of fire in the sky and pretended not to see them hesitantly moving closer.

All right, I had better break this awkwardness. I introduced myself to Inka, from Germany, Rico from Argentina, and Yoko from Japan. Neither spoke English well but they somehow found ways to communicate.

I opened my hands in an encircling motion, then pointed to the sand, the here and now. "How long?"

Inka, the red-haired girl, looked from the ocean to me. "Ten hours," she said and lifted her arms. "In the plane."

Giggles turned to laughter.

I pointed to the tents and all around the campgrounds. "How long have you been here?"

A short silence, then more laughter, until Yoko shook a head full of dark, straw-straight hair, and stuck out three fingers. "Three weeks." She nodded after every word.

"One month," Rico jumped in, his bright smile setting his bronzed skin aglow. "Almost. And two more coming."

Teenagers camping all summer long. Who knew there were parents as crazy as mine all over the world?

Willing or unwilling nature prisoners, we struck an immediate friendship. Curiosity found its way to my heart, sparked by the beautiful newness. A new adventure.

Sitting on the beach, we told stories in a mixture of English and quickly improvised sign language. Inka, the exchange student, was vacationing with her family visiting from Munich. Rico had finally made it to visit his sister, who worked as a Spanish teacher, and Yoko took English as a second language in hopes of being admitted at the Cal Arts Institute. I taught them unique English words like humongous, and learned how to say sea and wind in their languages.

Every evening, exhausted by our linguistic

shortcomings, we lay on the sand and counted the stars.

What started as sensory and stimulation withdrawal turned into a heightened awareness of the elements. We listened to the lapping of the waves, whispering its language or that of so many creatures inhabiting the ocean. In our silly minds, we tried to decide if the last whistling came from a dolphin or some other fish. We laughed so much.

Then, on the last day of the second week, it happened.

Two drops fell from the sky, stinging my arms. I should have hurried earlier. I should have run to the tent, but Inka was telling a story about liverwurst pate, the Christmas delicacy in her homeland.

Mom's non-existent California summer rain was upon us.

How could rain be so cold in the middle of summer? It hurt like ice needles poking the skin. Furious downpour drenched everything in five minutes. Soon, the dark clouds rolled away, casting strange shadows across the landscape.

The hot sun of the perfectly imperfect summer melted all anger and crippling fear of boredom into fun and peace. Far from home, with no connection to the world as I knew it, burried by books and serenaded by dolphin songs, I made new friends; and my summer, with its startling cold rain and blistery hot days, was perfect.

Thank you, Mom.

Le Bal des Abeilles
A.A Schenna

Chapter One

"I'm gonna getcha!" the woman crackled, her hands outstretched like a creepy witch. She followed after the little girl, pretending that she couldn't get closer to her.

"No, you will not!"

Brooke loved spending her time with her niece and it was obvious that she looked forward to playing their favorite game again with Joan. She enjoyed sharing carefree moments with the blonde angel who had stolen her heart, and moreover, it was her only chance to get past her fears and agony.

For the last three weeks, they would run into the house, screaming and trying to avoid one another's attack. The little girl rushed to escape, thinking of her options since she could either go straight under the huge, black table or toward the large, white sofa and hide behind it. The spacious living room was the best place for pillow fights and they both seemed eager to keep on having fun.

Brooke was really happy and looked impatient to getting her life back. She had started making thoughts and plans for the future, considering the possibilities of having her own family, and this time, she was sure she would make it.

The terrifying feeling of flirting intensely with death in her late thirties had vanished, and now she looked forward to living her life again. She was thirty-eight, but she didn't care about her age and the way she would look in the future. She had managed to reconsider the real meaning of life and respect the privilege of coming across the daylight every day that passed by.

"I need a break," Brooke said as she tried to catch her breath.

"Are you okay?" Joan was seven years old and looked like a beautiful doll. Her blonde, curly hair and her big, blue eyes showed off her sweet appearance.

"I am fine, Joan, but I think we should hurry up and fix everything because your mom is going to be here in a few minutes and we have a lot to do." Brooke looked around her and so did Joan.

"I will help you out," Joan whispered.

They rushed to fix the mess while accusing, teasing and laughing at one another for their careless behavior. Brooke was trying to clean the chips and the chocolate from the white carpets as Joan was dealing with the chaos in the kitchen, blaming her aunt for everything.

"Next time we will order Chinese food." Joan intoned as she took a few more steps and knelt, staring at her aunt.

"Are you crazy? Who's going to clean the rice from the carpets?" Brooke answered and looked Joan into her tiny eyeballs, waiting to see her beautiful smile.

"You will clean everything," the girl murmured and Brooke held her hands and locked her niece in her arms, biting softly her neck.

"I love you so much," the skinny woman said.

"I love you too, Brooke." Joan hugged tight her aunt and didn't have the least-intention of letting her go.

"I am glad you didn't call me aunt."

"You are my second mom and I love you so much," Joan whispered while she stretched out her arms to make her aunt see that she would always have her love and hugs. At the same time, a torrent of tears made its appearance on Brooke's pale face, flooding her heart and soul with hope and euphoria.

"You are my precious baby," she said

Her niece looked back at the door. "I think I heard the elevator," Joan exclaimed and stood up.

"Oh no...!" The woman sounded like a little girl too.

"Red alert, mom is here, I repeat, mom is here." They always had a great time together.

"Go to bed and pretend you are sleeping—otherwise your mom will kill us both." Brooke said, smiling at her niece.

***

"How are you?" Mel caressed her sister's back as she stood in front of the large door of the living room.

"I'm fine, Mel." Brooke sounded nervous.

"In a few months, everything will be different." Mel truly believed her words, and loved seeing her sister in her house.

"I know that, Mel." Brooke kept looking outside.

"Then why are you sad?" Mel said angrily.

"I don't like this weather. I miss the sun and the heat!" Brooke said. Mel smiled and hugged her older sister.

Although she knew what could still make her sister worry, she didn't say anything else about her behavior and cheerless mood. They stood at the windows, but both looked impatiently to the coming of summer and the high temperatures as well.

The view from the fifth floor was amazing and they could see everything covered by the snow. The streets, the trees, the cars and the signs were not visible anymore and the countless snowflakes wouldn't stop covering everything.

The severe winter had made everyone stay at home and they were all really angry about that. The majority of the residents of the small town were trapped behind the walls without having the comfort to accomplish all those they wanted and needed to do. Everyone had a bad case of cabin fever.

The last two months, Brooke had had to remain inside the house and avoid getting ill since she needed rest, and of course time to forget the adventure she had experienced. The bad weather didn't help at all.

"Let's talk about the summer holidays." Mel held her sister's hand and then they both headed toward the fireplace.

"What do you mean?" Brooke sounded serious.

"What are your plans for this summer? Mel asked.

"I have no plans," Brooke said vaguely.

"I see." Mel shook her head and smiled.

As usual, they kept talking for the whole night of many things while the snowflakes and the extremely low temperatures carried on turning the whole state into a frozen wasteland.

Chapter Two

Brooke and Mel walked down the streets, making plans for the weekend. The heat and the sun had brought the light and the carefree mood back in their lives, whereas the beautiful roses and the smell of the grass outside the small, white houses helped them dream of the best vacations they had lived, and wait patiently for the next weeks.

The last days of May were amazing since the high temperature during the daylight and the shinning stars during the nights had made everyone's wish come true, pushing everyone into taking the next step, dealing with the preparations for the upcoming summer days. The residents of the small town loved gardening, having their houses neat and painting their old furniture.

The two sisters didn't stop waving at the kind people while asking questions about their plans and projects. One aged couple loved spending their time at home, joking while tidying the garden and painting the huge pots for their new colorful flowers.

When Brooke knelt on the ground and smelled the yellow roses, she rolled her eyes and thought about how lucky she was.

A few meters further, a young couple had decided to clean the small pool and had already placed the big table and the comfortable chairs at their backyard again.

"It's so beautiful!" Brooke said.

"Yes, it is," Mel smiled at her sister and pointed at the house opposite them.

A young boy was playing with his dog while his parents didn't stop looking at their son, feeling happy and proud of their only child.

"Watch out!" Brooke held her sister's hand and dragged her to the sidewalk.

"I'm sorry!" a girl shouted out.

Brooke and Mel stood still, gazing at the children who kept running with their bicycles, showing off their skills in an effort to steal the admiration and the attention of the small neighborhood.

"I love summer!" Brooke said.

"Me too!" Mel was happy for many reasons.

The following weeks, the two sisters along with Joan didn't stop having fun and going out.

Brooke was healthy; she could touch her skin and feel beautiful again since her blonde hair had started making their appearance on her head, while her complexion had become the same as it was used to be, making her an attractive, sweet woman.

The nightmare was gone, she had won the worst enemy of her entire life, and now she felt ready to accept the new challenges that would come up. The following months she would have to abstain from anything stressful and she felt guilty for not helping her sister with their family business. On the other hand, Mel was clear and had warned her sister many times. *"You better stay at home and have fun—otherwise I will close the café and come over there to show you who the boss is."*

Brooke rubbed her eyes and smiled as she waited for her sister and Joan to put on their clothes and go out to watch the fireworks.

***

The beautiful square had everything anyone could imagine since they could see countless local products, books, drinks, and clothes. The traditional local festival of happiness had made everyone celebrate the arrival of summer, while the wind of change had brought the path of calmness closer to their lives.

Brooke looked happier than ever as Mel kept admiring her sister for her spirit and energy. Out of the blue, she grabbed her sister's hand and along with Joan, they started dancing, challenging the rest of the people to do the same thing.

In a few minutes, more than two hundred people were dancing and laughing, forming a chain where the positive energy was able to defeat everything sad and take the ghastly mood away.

"I have a surprise for you," Mel said, dancing with her sister.

"I hate surprises, so tell me now," Brooke said with a little laugh.

"I will not tell you yet," Mel answered seriously.

"Oh, come on, Mel." Brooke looked impatient.

"I will tell you anything you need to know in two days," Mel said, looking away and increasing her sister's curiosity.

"I could bite you like a vampire!" Brooke said. Mel started laughing at her and showing her her teeth.

Chapter Three

"Are you joking?" Brooke was surprised.

"No, I am not." Mel looked into her big eyes and then held her sister's head, touching noses with her.

"Can we afford this?" Brooke asked seriously.

"Listen to me, Brooke. I want you to go there and have fun." Mel was serious too and meant every single word.

"Thank you, Mel." Brooke nodded at her sister and hugged her tight.

"Enjoy your trip!" Mel said as she walked to the door.

"I will!"

"And have sex with someone you like!" Mel shouted as she closed the door behind her, leaving her sister alone, making dreams.

***

The moment Brooke got off the plane and stepped in the airport, she couldn't control her feelings. She started dancing and waving rhythmically at the beautiful women.

Being on vacation in Hawaii has always been her secret desire and now that she was there. She would do anything to have fun and seal the memories in her mind forever.

When she got in the taxi and looked at her watched the beautiful lei and smelled the colorful flowers, she smiled and felt wonderful. She had everything she wanted and looked forward to dancing the hula, the traditional dance of the magic islands.

On her way to the hotel, Brooke was able to see the huge, green mountains, the sun and the peaceful sky. The smell of the coconut trees along with the scent of the suntan oil made her soul rest in paradise. She rolled her eyes and thanked God for saving her life and for giving her the best sister in the world.

"Aloha!" the taxi driver said.

"Aloha!" she whispered as she waved at the polite, middle-aged driver.

Brooke walked toward the reception of the hotel and seemed impatient to change her clothes; she wanted to get rid of the tight white jeans and her white t-shirt. Being in Hawaii meant nothing but fun, swimsuit, sun oil, sunglasses and intense desire to flirt with life.

***

The following hours, Brooke looked completely different and seemed to enjoy herself. Although her skin had turned red, she kept strolling on the white beach and feeling the hot, white sand on her feet, brushing her blonde hair away from her face, happy it was long again. She was as beautiful as she used to be in the past and wasn't willing to waste her time as well.

The black swimsuit showed off her curves while the big, white hat and the silver bracelets on both her wrists and ankles made her look like a celebrity, maybe an actress who needed time to have some rest and leave everything behind.

When she closed her cell phone and thanked her sister yet again, she walked to the hotel, looking around her and thinking of her options and plans for her first night in the island of seduction. She was staying for five days in paradise and she didn't want to miss anything.

The exotic beach-bar near the wooden sidewalk stole her attention and, immediately, Brooke smiled as she already knew what she would do afterwards. She decided to have some rest and come back at the beach later to taste the famous cocktails and maybe to meet the love of her life.

Chapter Four

Brooke took off her white heels and held them with her right hand, impatient to reach the beach-bar and have some fun. The stars and the heat along with the beautiful music triggered her intention to do anything to feel amazing. After an incredible dinner, she wanted to dance, drink and meet new people.

Brooke wore a long colorful skirt and a small white top, leaving her back and her arms uncovered. The pink lipstick, her big, green eyes and her curly hair made her look fabulous, the consummate female who looked for joy, respect and love.

"Brooke!"

The woman turned back and smiled.

"Justin!" Brooke was surprised.

"What are you doing here?" the man asked.

"I was going to ask you the same thing!" Brooke said with a little laugh.

"I decided to thank myself for being a nice man, so I took the plane and came here to have some rest." Justin stared at her and laughed.

"Mel wanted to give me a gift, so I am here because of my sister."

"That's great," Justin said sincerely. He couldn't take his eyes off of her.

"Yea, I think it's great too," Brooke said softly, and smiled.

They walked to the bar and drank the famous cocktails while talking about their lives and childhood. They had known one another since they were children and there was always something between them.

***

The night Brooke along her sister and Joan went to the festival, Mel watched them talking and realized they were meant to be together. They were both acting weird and seemed shy while doing their best to coming up many subjects to keep on talking.

Later that night, Mel approached Justin and learned about his vacations, and didn't lose her time. The following day she arranged everything concerning her sister's trip to Hawaii since she knew what her sister was missing.

Mel was sure that Brooke needed a partner in her life, a serious man to hold her hand and reassure her that everything would be good. And the owner of the small book store was the perfect match for her sister.

Justin was in his early forties, single, handsome, smart and extremely kind with women. And he also seemed to be crazy in love with Brooke, as he was there for her and never stopped asking about her condition when she was fighting for her life. He never gave up on her and didn't move on, although many women liked him and used to flirt with him.

***

"I like your shirt." Brooke said.

"Are you kidding me?" Justin asked while staring at his colorful shirt.

"It looks like my skirt." Brooke smiled and so did he.

"Do you want it?" Justin asked.

"Yea, it would be perfect." Brooke laughed at him while Justin unbuttoned and took off his shirt.

"It's yours." Justin covered her back as Brooke gazed at his body.

"Let's go to the beach," she said.

They spent the rest of the night on the beach talking about their lives, staring at the ocean and sipping their drinks. They loved being there together, but they were both hesitant to make the next step as well.

The flames of the large torches around the beach-bar and along the beachfront added to the romantic tension as the atmosphere started becoming more erotically charged.

"We are in Hawaii and I think I want to do something crazy," Brooke whispered.

"What do you mean?" Justin asked as Brooke looked around her.

"I want to swim naked," Brooke murmured.

"I think it's a great idea," Justin sounded impatient and delighted.

Brooke got up and took off her clothes while Justin watched. When she got into the water, Justin took off his clothes too and followed her in.

The following minutes they came closer and left their bodies and minds free as the moonlight continued enlightening the peaceful surface of the ocean.

Chapter Five

"*Le bal des abeilles...*" Justin whispered.

"What does that mean?" Brooke looked into his big blue eyes and waited for his answer.

They were sitting on a bench, sharing glimpses of love and respect, watching Joan who loved making circles with her bicycle.

When Justin mentioned the dancing of the bees, Brooke smiled at her partner and leaned to his chest. As he held her tight, she thought of his words and tried to hide the tears of happiness and relief.

During the spring, the younger bees along with the new queen leave their nest behind and move on to better places to make a new beginning. When they do that, they start dancing in the air while looking forward to settling into their new home.

Brooke had managed to make a new beginning as well since she had a new partner and was healthy.

***

Immediately after their amazing vacations, Justin and Brooke came back home and shared countless lovely moments and unforgettable nights.

The first days of August were incredible since every night they used to go out and eat ice cream, watch movies at the beautiful open cinema of the small town and do many other simple things that demanded nothing but cheerfulness and interest.

They used to spend their weekends strolling around the lakes and the valleys while caressing the horses of their best friends. Horseback riding was really cool.

Justin knew Brooke loved reading romance novels and every night he used to bring her home the books of her favorite authors. He would never forget the moments they were sitting in the yard drinking lemonade and eating apple pie.

And they would never forget the lovely trip to Hawaii which brought them closer and made them realize that they were meant to be together.

Frozen Heart: Summer Thaw
K.C. Sprayberry

Chapter One

My ice skates safely tucked into their hard-sided bag, I walk out of the locker room. My mind whirls with all that I have to do before the big regional meet in a little less than two months, right before I start my senior year of high school. One thing I know that I can count on. I have no worries about anything preventing me from doing what had kept me sane the last seventeen years, eleven months, twenty-three days.

Well, it has actually only been fifteen years, eleven months, and twenty-three days. I didn't begin ice skating until I was two. And I can't wait to do regionals, even though the weather outside is hotter than hot, hot enough to as my dad loves to say, "fry an egg on the sidewalk." Although why anyone would want to do that, I have no clue. Sounds pretty stupid to me. Then again, my dad is always suggesting dumb stuff, as if that will make up all the times he has totally messed up my life.

Wonder if we'll go out to Grandma's in California after regionals? We'll have lots of time. School won't start for a week after that. Maybe we can go to Disneyland again.

Out the door in a flash, I scan the parking lot for Mom's totally cool Ford Fusion Energy Titanium. I convinced my parents to go with the black, and all the accessories. It was the first time ever we'd had a new car and I wanted something nobody would call bogus at school. Needless to say, on the few occasions I get to drive, everyone announces that I have my cool on.

I do have my cool on! Only a little over a year until I graduate. Then it's off to college in California, near Grandma. I can't believe that I got accepted to Stanford!

I received acceptances to every college I'd applied to—about twenty. Mom and Dad insisted on that many, so I wouldn't be limited in my choices if my dream college turned me down. But my dream college didn't turn me down, and even better, they accepted my guy, Tony Guillermo, too. We have so many plans for California, the first being finding an off-campus apartment as soon as we can without our parents blowing a cork.

See, my dad is a non-com, a non-commissioned officer. That's just a fancy name meaning that he's a Senior Master Sergeant in charge of the Deputy Commander for Maintenance's Admin section. Tony's dad is a pilot, an officer, and the kids aren't supposed to get close if their dads are officer and non-com.

Big whoop. We're more than friends and have been for a long time. Not that we've had sex yet—we're waiting. Shudder. Shudder. Shudder. I won't do that until I'm married. Don't want to end up like Mom and Dad, having to give up my dreams because a baby is about to show up, and then having to get married so everyone on base doesn't point fingers at us and whisper about how our parents can't "control" us.

Nope, not going to have a baby until I have my Marine Biology doctorate. Then babies are still a long time off, while Tony and I travel all over the place studying the environmental impact on marine animals.

"Blaire!" Mom waves at me from the side of a... a...

My jaw hits the ground, cracking and almost giving me a third degree burn. I can't believe what I'm seeing.

What is she driving? Why? That monster will totally destroy my cool!

My mom, Chelsea Thompson, is beside... I blink my eyes and then rub them to make sure I'm seeing right... a Ford Expedition. The largest, most uneconomical, environmentally unfriendly piece of junk that I've ever encountered!

"Coming." My heart sinks to the bottom of my feet.

I can just guess what she'll slip into our conversation on the way home.

No way! Not happening. I won't move. I'm not giving up ice skating, my guy, Dysart High, my guy, the friends I've had for three years, my guy. Did I mention my guy? I won't leave him, no matter how much I have to fight for the right to stay right here in Litchfield Park, Arizona, all by my lonesome!

She gets into the green—*pukey color*—Expedition and watches me approaching the SUV like it's a rattlesnake about to sink its fangs into my leg.

Through the not-tinted-for-Phoenix-summer windows I catch a glimpse of boxes and what looks like enough sports bags to outfit the whole base. My heart sinks lower, if that's even possible, as I realize all the hushed conversations between Mom and Dad, the nights I had to babysit eight-year-old Emily instead of going out with Tony, the abruptly interrupted phone calls when I walked into a room mean only one thing.

We are moving to another base.

I won't ask. I dump my skate bag in front of the passenger seat, get in, and buckle up. *I'm going to make both of them sweat. No way am I leaving high school less than a year before I graduate!*

Chapter Two

Mom starts the engine and then peers at me.

"Good practice?" she asks.

"It was a practice."

I'm nowhere near ready to let her off the hook, allowing her to get away with not telling me this months ago. Is she stupid? Doesn't she get that I know she and Dad knew about what she's about to announce at least before Valentine's Day. Doesn't she get that I recognize all the signs she's about to screw up my life in a major way?

"I have a date with Tony in a couple of hours." My tone is surly, my attitude even worse.

"Uh, honey." She pulls out into traffic and drives away from home. "I hate to tell you this, but your daddy got a short notice assignment. You know what that means."

I inhale deeply through my nose, making sure that is as noisy as possible. Yeah, I know what that means, but it's not happening. Does anyone up there hear me? It is just plain not happening. No way!

Not only does this announcement screw up regionals, which I have practiced for forever, it will also mess up all the plans I have with my friends—a Grand Canyon day trip without parents, hanging around Sedona, visiting Tombstone, a camping trip to the Petrified Forest, and the concerts. Oh, the bands that will be coming to Phoenix this year are the absolute best, and I will not miss a single appearance!

"So?"

Rudeness. That's good. Be rude. Be obnoxious. Let her figure out that I will not let her and Dad off the hook so easily. I mentally search my uber-long list of friends, trying to figure out just one whose parents define cool, who won't care about another teenage girl in the house for a few measly months. I can spend holidays and vacations with Grandma if need be. She's always asking Mom and Dad to let me come out on my own. I can even talk Mom into getting that ultra-cool Fusion back, so I have a car.

"Please don't be like this, Blaire," Mom begs. "Your dad and I are well aware of what this means to you." She peeks at me out of the corner of her right eye. "There's a skating rink at the new base."

I tap a foot against the floorboard of this decidedly environmentally unfriendly monster SUV. My lips remain closed. If Dad were around, he'd make some snarky comment about finally having peace, but he doesn't ever remember this is my warning that I'm about to explode all over everyone.

"I'm sure you'll find lots of new friends in Moose Creek." She keeps talking like this is a normal conversation, about a vacation, or a student exchange program. "Emily and Ricky are overjoyed that we're going up there. We've never lived in that part of the country."

Clue 1: We're not leaving the United States. Still, Moose Creek doesn't sound like it's in Arizona.

"Not going," I mutter under my breath.

"Oh, you are going." Mom stops at a red light and turns to look at me. "You're going with a smile on your face, ready to take on a new school and find new friends." She faces the traffic right as the light turns green. "I will not put up with one of your temper tantrums."

"Where is this Moose Creek?" I go for more ammunition to point out how horrible she's being by making me move away from my friends.

"Alaska. Near Fairbanks."

"Alaska?" I scream in horror. "Are you freaking kidding me?"

The cars start moving. Mom's first off the line, like she's in some kind of race. The sound of a whole lot of tires scraping roadway, a loud air horn blasting a warning that's too late, makes me turn my head. All I can see is a red semi smashing into Mom's side of the Expedition.

We're spinning, being hit over and over again. The front of the SUV crumples. Searing pain rips up and down my right knee.

A piercing wail rips out of my throat after I force my head around to look at Mom. The whole driver's side is mashed down on top of her. All I can see are the fingers of one of her hands, stretched toward me.

Chapter Three

We didn't leave for Alaska the night my whole life was destroyed. That happens today, after Dad signs out from the base. Today happens to be a month after our whole world turned upside down, when a semi driver ran a red light and killed Mom. Today also happens to be my eighteenth birthday, but I threatened to run away (as if I can, stuck like I am in this stupid thing) if anyone even mentions "Happy Birthday."

I never knew how much it would hurt not to have her around all the time. Of course, I haven't had as bad a time as Ricky and Emily. Ricky had to be the man of the house while Dad was at the base. My little brother is fifteen, a freshman at Dysart, and really wants to get away from Phoenix as fast as possible. Emily had her ninth birthday the day I was released from the hospital, a mere ten days ago. We had her party at a Chuck E. Cheese, but even with all her friends around, it was a total bummer. Em did nothing but cry, even when the character mouse brought out her cake and ice cream. I had a hard time pretending that I didn't care about any of it. There's a massive hole in my heart, and not just because that stupid driver killed my mom.

"Okay, kids." Dad parks near the building where he used to work. "We only have to stay here for about ten, maybe twenty minutes. A lot of people want to say goodbye to us. They've been real good to our family since the... accident." He glances at me. "So, put up with it. We'll be on the way to Sky Harbor Airport soon and you'll never have to think about Phoenix again."

A massive lump clogs my throat, making my chest hurt. Tony hasn't shown up since the accident. He hasn't even called. I'm pretty sure his dad won't be here, since he's a pilot and my dad works in maintenance.

"Blaire." Dad opens the door beside me. "Don't

tense up, honey. I'm still learning how to do this."

His warning doesn't ease the other pain killing me on the inside. Both of my legs are in casts, a result of the accident. My right knee will have to be replaced sometime in the future; my left fibula fractured when something in the wreck smashed against it. I don't get to think about crutches for at least another month.

One of his arms supports my back and the other gently lifts my legs out. For the first time since a therapist showed him how to ease me into a wheelchair, Dad does it right.

"Okay?" he asks.

"Sort of." I brush away a tear.

Em and Ricky join us. She tugs at my right arm.

"Can I ride in your lap, Blaire? Please?"

I want to scream no. I've been doing that since the doctor let her into my room at the hospital, but her little face is so gloomy. Em's a smiler, a happy girl, but not since her mommy didn't come home. I think back to when I was her age, having to move and not knowing what I'd find in our new home.

Yeah. I felt pretty much the same way she does. Or not. I always had Mom around.

I hold out my arms and shake as I lift Em onto my lap. Dad makes a move to help but then he grasps the handles at the back of the wheelchair, waits for me to settle Em, and starts us moving toward the double glass doors.

Thanks, Dad, for not making a huge deal out of this. I decide I'll say that to his face after we get to Alaska tonight.

"Surprise!"

The shouts from those Dad has worked with since we arrived here startle me for a second. Em starts crying, not that I blame her. Surprises aren't much fun without Mom around. We used to depend on her to keep us on an even keel, whenever Dad's duties took him from us for months on end.

Who will do that now?

The question bothers me long after we leave Luke Air Force Base for the last time and board our plane to Alaska.

Chapter Four

Five and a half hours later, one change of planes, and we're in Alaska. There's a coldness to the air that I expected, no snow thankfully, and an extraordinarily weird event going on—it's still daylight, as in middle of the day daylight.

"It's ten at night. What's going on?" Ricky asks.

For a boy, he's really very quiet, and has gotten more that way since we lost Mom. I kind of wish I could tell him what it is. I'd like to know myself, but I never bothered to study all the literature we got from Dad's sponsor about this area.

Wish I had now. That looks totally cool.

"The sun doesn't go all the way down up here until September." A tall, hunky guy my age strolls over to us. "Senior Master Sergeant Thompson?" he asks. "I'm Gerry Anderson. Mom got called back on duty. Some kind of problem with the latest Red Flag exercise."

Gerry. Hunky guy's name is Gerry. Cool.

The "it's always summer time in Phoenix" beckoning call that's been on me since I learned about this assignment begins to fade. Sure, it's nice, almost like summer, in the Valley of the Sun most of the time, and I do have a guy that I promised to miss every second of the day and night, but right in front of me is a prime example of hunkyness that I can't ignore.

"That's me." Dad juggles our carry-on luggage, finally dropping all but one bag, the one containing all the meds and other necessities I need until the casts come off. "What's up on the base?"

He holds out a hand and shakes the one Gerry offers, like they're buds or equals in the military. I'm very impressed. This is the first time my dad has ever treated a guy my age the same way he does the people in the Air Force.

"Some fool pilot ran off the runway on takeoff." Gerry grins. "Happens at least twice every Red Flag."

In the distance, I can hear the high-pitched whine of a fighter jet preparing for takeoff. Ricky glances in that direction, a look of yearning on his pimply face. He's wanted to go to the Air Force Academy since he was like five, and if nothing else bad happens, he might just get the chance. Like me, he has astral grades, and is involved in extra-curricular activities.

Doesn't look like I'll have a chance at my extra-curricular activities any time soon. It'll take years to get my knee fixed, if ever.

Pity wells up within me, wiping away most of the positive feelings I had once we landed. I'm missing Tony, my friends at Dysart High, the warm weather, even Mom nagging me to do something.

"Your mom sent me a message but I haven't had time to read it yet," Dad says. "I hope nothing has gone wrong."

"Nothing big." Gerry's face twists into partial grief, and partial anger. He turns away from us. "Nothing a miracle won't cure."

So the hunky guy has a secret, and he looks so sweet when he's sad. Of course, I'm unhappy that he's so upset, but he seems a lot more reachable this way. Kind of like that puppy dog we had to leave in Germany.

"Maybe if you talk about it, things won't be so bad," I say. "That's what Dad has been telling me since the—" My tongue sticks to the roof of my mouth for a second. "—accident."

Gerry glances at me. He looks me up and down. I'm sorry now that I didn't take the flight attendant's offer to help me freshen up before we arrived. My brandy brown hair is probably a fright, to say nothing of how greasy my face is.

"How did you manage to break both legs?" he

finally asks.

"Wreck." I choke back tears. "Left ankle and right knee broken. Well, the knee is totally trashed. I might have to have it replaced."

"Oh." His head drops and he stares at the floor. "That was you."

Now I'm really mystified. What was me? How can he know about a wreck in Phoenix all the way up in Alaska? It's not like it made the national news or anything.

"Ricky, grab the luggage tags and have Gerry show you where to get our bags." Dad picks up Em and sets her in my lap gently. "Did General Hopkins get permission for you to park near the luggage area, Gerry?"

"Sure did." Gerry points toward a door near us. "Truck's right out there. Here." He hands Dad a set of keys. "Get on in and settle. Won't take us but a minute." He glances at Ricky. "Grab a trolley. We'll pick up your bags and get to Moose Creek fast."

Dad pushes me toward the door. Em leans against me and is snoring softly before we get outside.

"Don't push Gerry for information," Dad says, stopping in front of an even bigger SUV than the one Mom was driving *that* day. "Let me settle Em, and then if there's time, I'll explain while I get you into this monster." He grins. "I thought I got a big enough SUV to handle the winters around here. Guess I should have checked out this one."

A couple of minutes later, he squats by the still open door, his hands checking out the casts and my toes, to be certain nothing is going wrong.

"Blaire, I know you're still upset about leaving your friends and coming up here," he says. "I figure the whole reason you don't want to talk to me about the wreck is that you and your mom were arguing right before it happened."

I nod.

"Honey, your mom and I talked about letting you

stay behind, but just about everyone we know, the parents of most of your friends, got orders. They're going all over the place. I'm the only person who is staying in CONUS."

I know that CONUS means Continental United States, but the rest of what he's saying is a huge news break. None of my friends said a word.

"Why?"

"Needs of the military." He scrubs his hands over his face. "Okay, here's the bad news, and I knew it before we came up here. You can yell at me later, but remember, you can't yell at Gerry or blame him. It's not his fault."

I listen in horror as my dad talks about how sometimes parents are the ones who need to grow up, and how Gerry and his mom had a great assignment to Germany cancelled because of something his dad did... in Phoenix. With growing anger, I realize what that something was and want to run away as far as I can. But I can't, because of the stupid casts and wheelchair.

"Gerry's dad hit Mom and me?" I ask before Dad finishes.

"Yes, honey." He clasps my suddenly cold hands. "He was drunk. There's some speculation that he spent a lot of time that way, but he hadn't been in Gerry's life for a couple of years, not since his wife re-upped and he got out."

The first emotion rising to the surface is anger. Deep seated rage. All I want to do is make sure Gerry feels exactly like I do.

"And you're telling me this why?" I ask.

"Because Gerry is going to the Air Force Academy next year," Dad says. "You know how much Ricky is looking forward to applying there."

I stare at my hands, curled into fists. The rage intensifies. Gerry doesn't have to give up his dreams because his dad murdered my mom and destroyed my dreams. Sure, he can't go to the new base, but he still has his mom while mine is in a casket thousands of miles away from where I am now.

"It's not fair." A tear slips out of my eye and slides along my nose. "It's just not fair."

"Life isn't fair," Dad says. "It never has been, and that's sure not going to change any time soon. Blaire, please, for everyone's sake, forgive Gerry. Not that you really need to, but I know how you think. He's a good kid with a dad who was trouble long before he illegally drove a semi into that SUV down in Phoenix."

I want to scream, sob out everything I remember from the wreck, all the rage I feel, but I can't. And that's for a very good reason. Gerry isn't his dad. He's not responsible for the constant pain I feel in my heart.

"I won't give him any grief," I say. "It's not his fault, Dad. It's probably more my fault, because, yeah, Mom and I were fighting. I didn't want to come here." I choke on a sob. "And now she's dead, and my whole life is ruined. I'll never skate again, never... never... never walk right, maybe never get to go to Stanford and become a Marine Biologist."

"You can be whatever you want to be." Dad pats my hand. "You have it in you, kiddo. You always were the strongest of my kids."

I don't get what he's saying, probably never will, but that doesn't matter. I've found a distraction in the form of a kid with the same issues I have. Maybe Gerry will help me figure out how to stop blaming myself for the wreck.

Chapter Five

A couple of days later, Gerry shows up first thing in the morning. Dad, Ricky, and Em spent that time making sure our house looks great. There's not much I can do until I'm out of at least one of the casts, and I won't even get an estimate of that until a doctor at Eilson's hospital has a chance to look over my medical records from Luke.

"What's happening?" Gerry sits beside me.

Well, he's in a comfy chair in the living room and I'm still in the wheelchair.

"Not much," I admit. "Just thinking about school, how I'll get around." *Liar!* "And about what everyone does in the winter around here. It's okay now, except for the sun being up twenty-four hours a day. And it's a lot colder than I expected. It's usually hot in Phoenix, summer time hot."

"So I hear." He grins. "Hot enough to fry eggs on the sidewalk."

"Nah, that's July."

"I'll remember that." His expression goes from interested to down in a funk in a second. "Mom talked to me this morning. About how your legs got messed up. I'm sorry."

"You weren't driving that semi." Despite my promise to Dad, it's really hard to say those words.

"She also told me that your dad believes you're blaming yourself for the accident." He stares at me. "Are you?"

"Kind of."

"Don't."

"Why not?"

"Cause it's not your fault. You weren't driving drunk. The light was green for you and your mom. My loser dad did what he does best, ruined everyone's life just so he can do what he wants." Gerry turns away for a second, wiping under his nose. "He's in jail. There's nobody willing to come up with fifty grand for bail, so that's where he'll stay until after the trial." He turns back to me. "And I hope he goes to prison for the rest of his loser life."

I'm in total awe of this guy. He's already told Dad that he'll make sure I stay caught up in my classes, even volunteered to take me to and from school, along with Ricky and Em. Gerry has done so much for my family, including offering to do our grocery shopping, a feat we'll attempt tonight at the base commissary.

"What's moose meat like?"

"Nasty." Gerry wrinkles his nose. "Why?"

"I was thinking of asking Dad to get some, so we can grill burgers." I smile, a real, genuine, teeth exposed smile. "Maybe you and your mom can come over for some. I can even make a potato salad and have Dad grill corn."

"Get some Angus beef," he suggests. "The commissary doesn't carry moose. Not sure why, but I'm sure glad they don't. I had that stuff once. It's bad enough to gag maggots."

We sit and talk for a couple of hours. Ricky reappears with Em around lunch time.

"Dad said we could make some of the frozen pizzas," Em says.

"How can Dad say that?" I ask. "He's at the base, signing in."

"He's home, Blaire," Ricky says. "His new boss gave him the rest of the week as compassionate leave, so he can set up your doctor's appointments and get us settled. We have to have a babysitter." He wrinkles his nose. "So there are no problems."

"Yeah." Gerry snorts with laughter. "Me. I'm the babysitter, and it's mostly so there's someone trained in first aid until Blaire is out of her casts."

"Really?" I grin at him. "Thanks."

Dad walks in with a bunch of grocery bags, jerking

his head at the still open door. "Get the rest of the groceries, Ricky. Em, help me put this stuff away." He grins at Gerry. "Glad you're here. I need to fill our propane tank."

Miracle of all miracles, thanks to some great planning by people at Luke, our household goods were shipped up here long before I got out of the hospital. The house looks like we live here, instead of just moved here.

That's good and bad. There are things that remind me of Mom every time I look at them, but then I think about all the good times, so I'm not so sad.

"Sure." Gerry goes to help Dad unpack the groceries. "I was just telling Blaire that we'll have a blast once school starts."

Not quite the truth, but this guy just impressed my dad. I lean against the back of the chair and lose myself in daydreams of sunlit midnight walks away from the base. A text alert interrupts my happiness.

Hey. Hope you're settling in. We're leaving for Spain in the morning. Mom convinced me to do college over there. See you someday. Tony.

"Jerk!" I delete every text from him, his phone number, and begin on all the pictures of us together. "Total jerk!"

Gerry peeks out of the kitchen doorway. "Problem."

Gorgeous hunkyness, I remind myself. Real, gorgeous hunkyness is here for me now. Who cares about Tony? He can stay in Spain for the rest of his life. I won't miss him... much.

Chapter Six

It's August. I've been in Alaska for almost two months, and my legs are finally cast free. I peek at them and groan at how pale they are. Usually, this time of year, I have a gorgeous tan, but not now.

"Cute." Gerry grins at me when I walk slowly out of the doctor's office on crutches. "I like."

"You would," I retort. "I'll never learn to use these."

"Sure you will." He opens the door for me. "It'll just take practice. Tell you what, let's go somewhere private and you can fall on your butt all you like until you master those sticks."

"You're on."

We get into his pickup. Well, he helps me in and then we're off on an adventure I wouldn't have looked forward to only a few months ago. Alaska has grown on me. It's so beautiful, so colorful. There's so much to see here, especially the Northern Lights which have yet to make their appearance, but that will happen once daylight stops being twenty-four hours a day, which according to Gerry is late next month.

"Ready?" He parks near a stream and comes around to help me out. "This is the best place around here."

I see what he means. There's a massive meadow of bright yellow flowers right in front of us. The aroma is wonderful. Hearing the stream trickling over rocks entices me to check it out, but I'm pretty sure it will be colder than I'm used to.

"Come on." Gerry points at the meadow. "It's really easy to walk through."

He matches his steps to mine and talks in a quiet voice as we move through the meadow. Most of what he's telling me has to do with how he and his mom have lived up here since he was in eighth grade. The assignment she lost because of his dad being a total jerk was one she'd wanted for years, but Gerry's pretty happy they're staying here.

"Mom retires next year," he says. "She's always loved Alaska. It would have been hard to move overseas and then come back so fast."

"The Air Force doesn't usually move someone so close to retirement," I say. "Dad explained to me how this is his last assignment, because he's retiring in a couple of years. But they can't have two people in charge of the section where he was assigned."

"They won't." Gerry helps me sit among the flowers. "Mom's working for the base commander now, as a liaison to the Red Flag personnel. It's a great transition for her, a new kind of job. She's really happy."

I catch a meaning behind those words, and it worries me. Gerry never talks about how he actually feels. It's his mom, or my dad, or the officers in charge of the base.

"What about you?" I ask.

"I'm not important."

His response bothers me on so many levels. Yeah, I was a total spoiled brat back in Phoenix. I get that now. It's easy to see that I wasn't thinking about our whole family, even though I thought I had a lot of good reasons, but I've learned a lot since the accident.

"Yes, you are." I face him. "We're all important. I didn't get that until my mom was gone. Look, I've never told anyone this, but it was… it was—"

I choke up, turn away from the one person I can trust, and stare at the deep blue sky. Somehow, it seems easier to talk to him this way.

"The cops in Phoenix still have to talk to me about the accident. I couldn't at the time. That's because I saw my mo… all I saw of my mom when everything stopped spinning were the fingers of one of her hands. She was reaching for me." My chest heaves from unshed tears. "Gerry, I was screaming at her right before it happened. I thought she and Dad wanted to ruin my life, and she reached for me instead of protecting herself."

Gerry slides a cautious arm around my shoulder. I lean against his shoulder, letting his comforting strength help with the feelings I still have.

"She loved you a lot." His voice is quiet, full of concern and I think a touch of admiration. "That's why she wanted to make sure you were okay."

"I get that." I point at my forehead. "Here, but my heart still hurts so much. I haven't been able to tell anyone this."

"I'm here for you any time."

I take his promise seriously. One thing I've learned about Gerry since meeting him—he will never tell someone something and then forget it. That's a lot better than what I had with Tony. Not long before my life fell apart, we were starting to move apart, but we wouldn't admit that to anyone. We were the dream team at Dysart High. Now, I know that it was natural for us to pull apart. Tony was so different from who I was. Gerry, he's a guy who treats me like I matter, like what I think is important. I didn't have that with Tony.

"Come on." He pulls me to my feet and helps me with the crutches. "How about if I teach you how to make Alaska chili?"

"What makes it different from regular chili?

"Moose meat."

I stare at him with my mouth hanging open. "You said that you hated moose meat."

"Not in chili."

We're laughing as we go back to his pickup. I'm liking this guy the more I spend time with him. He's pretty cool.

Chapter Seven

September arrives and the promise of normal day and night happens. Gerry and I have a lot of the same classes at school, and he goes out of his way to make sure I have a great time with the group of military kids who usually stick together.

One thing I notice about life in Alaska. Except for the major difference in the weather, it's pretty much like life in Phoenix, Germany, Spain, South Carolina, and every place I lived as a military brat. Not much changes, except the scenery, and here it's wild and sweet, gloriously colorful and occasionally filled with danger, yet it also feels safe.

"Ready for the game tonight." Gerry leans against my locker. "I'm starting."

"What position?"

"Uh…" He rubs the back of his neck. "Guy most likely to be on the bottom of the pile after a tackle."

"Good one." I laugh. "Seriously."

"Seriously. My dad guilted me into playing football. He called me a pansy when I said I'd rather take pictures from the sidelines."

"Why?" I can't believe what Gerry's telling me. No Dad I've ever known has treated their kid like this.

"He said only pansies didn't want to play football." He shrugs. "I'm not great, most of the team isn't, but we do have a lot of fun. Even if we don't win many games."

I still don't get something. Sure, I can't ice skate any longer, at least not in competition. That's the reality of what happened to my knee, but Gerry has a choice. He knows his dad will never come around again, so it doesn't make sense for him to stick with a sport he hates.

"You can quit, you know," I say, sounding more intense than I ever have before. "There's no reason you have to keep playing if you don't like it."

He snorts out a laugh. I don't get it. What's so funny?

"But I do have to stick with the team," Gerry says around bouts of laughter. "The team is really small. We barely have a second string, and they're all freshman. We wouldn't qualify for conference play if even one of us quits. That's why I stick with it."

"Oh!" Heat flashes across my face. I know I look like I just fell into a huge vat of ketchup. "Yeah. I did notice the school is pretty small."

"You gonna be out there tonight, to cheer for me whenever I get tackled?"

"Wouldn't miss it for the world."

***

The game ends just like Gerry predicted it would. The team lost in a spectacular manner, but I'm hoarse from cheering my guy every time he got tackled. It's so totally weird, but fun at the same time. He comes out from the showers and nods at the cars leaving the parking lot.

"We're meeting up at Charlie's Grilled Subs on base," he says. "Want to hang with me over there?"

That has to be the weirdest way I've ever been asked out, but it also feels comfortable, right. I nod and glance around for Dad. He's with Lillian, Gerry's mom, Ricky, and Em.

"See you at home," Dad calls. "Don't stay out too late."

That was way too easy. I didn't even have to ask.

Although a little worried about how easily Dad agreed to my unasked question, I ride with Gerry to the sub place. Once inside, we check out the menu. He orders a pepperoni steak sub, piled up with tons of onions and green peppers.

Good. I can have what I really like.

Another irritating thing about Tony. He was all into "I'm a vegan." without really knowing what all that entailed. Eating out with him was a total challenge, since I love my meat, and seeing that Gerry has ordered my second favorite sub, I go with my fav.

"The barbecue cheddar sub please." My mouth waters in anticipation of the grilled and crisp onions, all of the sandwich bathed in a spicy barbecue sauce and shredded cheddar. "Oh, and how about if we split an order of cheese and bacon fries?"

"Works for me." Gerry nods at the guy behind the counter. "And a couple of your blueberry lemonades."

"Yum." I lick my lips. It's like Gerry reads my mind. We are so on the same page. "Want to split half of our subs?"

"Yes!" He sounds like a kid standing in front of the candy counter. "Great. You totally rock, Blaire."

Later, after the subs are nothing more than some crumbs on the wrapping, we just stare at each other.

"I have something for you." Gerry pulls out a ring, but not just any old ring. It has a silver band with a rock in it that is a light purple with gold streaks running through it. "Just friends," he whispers, sliding it onto my left ring finger. "But I don't want to have to chase away the other guys."

Okay, I get why he's saying just friends. I agree. We just met a couple of months ago, and both of us have had a lot going on in our lives. I admire the ring and smile at him.

"Just friends." *For now.*

Chapter Eight

It's no longer daylight twenty-four hours a day. And it's still a bit colder than I like, but Gerry is teaching me a lot about Alaska. Especially about the great university in Anchorage. I've finally made my decision. I'll stay here, work on getting my knee back in shape, and help out Dad while Gerry goes into the Air Force.

The pretty ring on my finger, made from some kind of stone I've never seen before, seems to wink at me. We're not engaged, that's still a long way off, but we are committed. Turns out Dad was right all along. Kids who have non-coms for parents should never hang with officer's kids. It just doesn't work.

Gerry and I are in our favorite meadow, lying on our backs and watching the sky. Once darkness settles in, I can make out a ribbon of color waving from side.

"Ohhhhh!" I breathe in and out. "Is that it?"

"Northern Lights, Dad!" Em squeals nearby. "They're pretty."

"That's it." Gerry holds my hand tight. "Keep watching."

For the next hour, he and I watch those shining ribbons in many colors move across the sky, like waves in the ocean. Occasionally, I can hear Em squealing some more, or Ricky asking questions. Dad and Lillian are talking too.

Maybe Mom might have liked it up here, but I get what Dad's going through. He has to single parent three kids and has a very important job with the Air Force. Besides, Lillian is pretty cool.

Looks like Alaska is the happening place for us.

About the Authors:

S Cu'Anam Policar:

S.Cu'Anam Policar was born in Brooklyn, NY, but now lives in Missouri. The mother of three, she makes time to write, usually late at night.

An avid reader, she not only writes, but helps promote other authors with blog tours and reviews of their books.

She is Pagan but respects all religions and believes everyone should celebrate their similarities and not worry about their differences.

When she has the time, she enjoys playing video games, horseback riding, singing, and writing short stories.

Also the founder of Wolf Paw Publications, she believes quality work shouldn't cost an author an arm and leg. While her prices are competitive, the quality of her work shines through.

She absolutely loves to make new friends so don't be afraid to come by and say hi on Facebook!

Facebook: https://www.facebook.com/AuthorCuAnam

Twitter: https://twitter.com/CuAnam

Pinterest: https://www.pinterest.com/cuanam/

GoodReads:
https://www.goodreads.com/author/show/7126980.S_Cu_A nam_Policar

Margaret Egrot:

I have lived in The United Kingdom all my life. I have worked with the Probation Service, the Police Authority, as a Charity boss, and as a freelance child protection consultant. I currently sit on the boards of two charities: one that runs assessment centres for families experiencing problems, and one that provides services for the elderly (well, you've got to think ahead...)

I enjoy reading and the theatre. I try to keep fit by swimming and racing my cairn terrier round the park. He usually wins.

Facebook: https://www.facebook.com/pages/Margaret-Egrot/1374506486178952

Twitter: https://twitter.com/meegrot

Charmaine Pauls:

Charmaine Pauls was born in Bloemfontein, South Africa. She obtained a degree in Communications at University of Potchestroom, and followed a diverse career path in journalism, public relations, advertising, communications, photography, graphic design, and brand marketing. Her writing has always been an integral part of her professions.

After relocating to France with her French husband, she fulfilled her passion to write creatively full time. Charmaine has published six novels since 2011, as well as several short stories and articles.

When she is not writing, she likes to travel, read, and rescue cats. Charmaine currently lives in Chile with her husband and children. Their household is a linguistic mélange of Afrikaans, English, French, and Spanish.

Website: http://charmainepauls.com/
Facebook: https://www.facebook.com/pages/Charmaine-
Pauls/175738829145132
Amazon: http://www.amazon.com/Charmaine-
Pauls/e/B005LY9B82/ref=sr_tc_2_0?qid=1386597421&sr
=1-2-ent
Goodreads:
https://www.goodreads.com/author/show/5161287.Charmai
ne_Pauls
Twitter: https://twitter.com/CharmainePauls

Penny Estelle:

Penny Estelle is a best-selling writer for all ages, from the early reader to adult. Her books range from picture books for the little ones to fantasy and time travel adventures for ages 9 to 13. She also, under P.A. Estelle, has written adult stories, including a family drama and contemporary, paranormal, and historical western romances
Penny was a school secretary for 21 years. She and her husband moved to their retirement home in Kingman, AZ on a very rural 54 acres, living on solar and wind energy only.

Website: http://pennystales.com/
Blog: http://www.pennyestelle.blogspot.com/
Amazon: http://www.amazon.com/Penny-
Estelle/e/B006S62XBY

E.B. Sullivan

E.B. Sullivan is a clinical psychologist who loves to write fictional tales. She lives in California with her husband, dogs, cats, and horses. Elizabeth describes her life as a continuous and exciting adventure. Her other books under Solstice are the novels *Different Hearts*, *Bloom Forevermore*, *Grandfathers' Bequest*, and *Alaska Awakening*, and the novellas *Christmas Guardian Angel* and *Spotlighting Crime*.

Website: www.ebsullivan.com
Blog: http://www.ebsullivan.com/blog
Twitter: https://twitter.com/EBSullivan1
Facebook: https://www.facebook.com/ebsullivan1
Goodreads:
https://goodreads.com/author/list/7101680.E_B_Sullivan
Amazon: http://www.amazon.com/E.B.-Sullivan/e/B00895GBJC/ref=ntt_dp_epwbk_0

Barbra Weitzner:

Barbara Weitzner lives in Delray Beach, Florida with her husband. Her big loves are her family and football. She has been featured in Soundings Literary magazine and Breezes magazine. She is now at work on her second novel, A New Start. You can find her on Facebook and LinkedIn.

Cynthia Ley:

Cynthia Ley lives in the lower Pacific Northwest between volcanoes and the sea. She is the author of three short story collections: Perfect & Other Stories, Tales of a Twisted World, and Creeps & Creepers: Three Eerie Tales, and has contributed to several Solstice seasonal anthologies (The Food of Love; Summer Thrills, Summer Chills). Her titles, all published by Solstice, are available through Amazon.com.

Facebook: https://www.facebook.com/groups/cleyfiction4/

G-mail: Cjleyedit4@gmail.com

Twitter: https://twitter.com/CynthiaLey2

Or follow her on her blog at:

https://authorcjl.wordpress.com/

Silvia Villalobos:

Silvia Villalobos is a short-story writer and novelist. Her stories have appeared in various literary magazines, from Pure Slush to Red Fez. She is a native of Romania, who lives immersed in the laid-back vibe of California with her husband and son.

Blog: https://silviatomasvillalobos.wordpress.com/

Facebook: https://www.facebook.com/silvia.villalobos.140

Twitter: https://twitter.com/Silvia__Writes

Google+: https://plus.google.com/u/0/115354555498756576045/posts

Website: http://www.strangerorfriend.com/

A.A. Schenna:

As a child, A.A dreamed of being a cardiac surgeon. Later, he realized that this was not what he wanted.

Writing has always been his greatest pleasure. When he doesn't write action, adventure, romance stories or anything else, he reads everything.

Schenna admires all the writers he comes across and enjoys talking about books and magazines.

A.A loves meeting new people and discovering new places. Trapped in Timelessness, Lake's Curse, The Alphas, Limitless Love Collection, On the Sixth Floor are available through the Solstice Publishing website.

Website: www.aaschenna.com

Facebook: https://www.facebook.com/pages/AA-Schenna/701740166542505?ref=hl

Twitter: https://twitter.com/ASchenna

K.C. Sprayberry:

Born and raised in Southern California's Los Angeles basin, K.C. Sprayberry spent years traveling the United States and Europe while in the Air Force before settling in Northwest Georgia. A new empty nester with her husband of more than twenty years, she spends her days figuring out new ways to torment her characters and coming up with innovative tales from the South and beyond.

She's a multi-genre author who comes up with ideas from the strangest sources. Some of her short stories have appeared in anthologies, others in magazines. Three of her books (Softly Say Goodbye, Who Am I?, and Mama's Advice) are Amazon best sellers. Her other books are: Take Chances, Where U @, The Wrong One, Pony Dreams, Evil Eyes, Inits, Canoples Investigations Tackles Space Pirates, Canoples Investigations Versus Spacers Rule, The Call Chronicles 1: The Griswold Gang, The Curse of Grungy Gulley, Paradox Lost: Their Path, Starlight, Soar High 1: Standing Strong, and Lost & Scared. Additionally, she has shorts available on Amazon: Grace, Secret From the Flames, Family Curse … Times Two, Right Wrong

Nothing In Between, Love Anew, Last Chance, and The Ghost Catcher.

Facebook: http://www.facebook.com/pages/KC-Sprayberry/331150236901202
Twitter: https://twitter.com/kcsowriter
Blog: http://outofcontrolcharacters.blogspot.com/
Website: www.kcsprayberry.com
Goodreads: http://www.goodreads.com/author/show/5011219.K_C_Sprayberry
Amazon: http://www.amazon.com/-/e/B005DI1YOU
Google +: https://plus.google.com/u/0/+KcSprayberry/posts
Pinterest: http://pinterest.com/kcsprayberry/boards/
Authorgraph: http://www.authorgraph.com/authors/kcsowriter
Amazon book list: http://www.amazon.com/s/ref=nb_sb_noss_1?url=search-alias%3Ddigital-text&field-keywords=k.c.%20sprayberry&sprefix=k.c.+%2Cdigital-text
Manic Readers: http://www.manicreaders.com/KCSprayberry/
AUTHORSdb http://authorsdb.com/authors-directory/5230-k-c-sprayberry
AUTHORSdb listing: http://authorsdb.com/show-all-my-listings

42850360R00093

Made in the USA
Charleston, SC
09 June 2015